I

So many things, so many things can happen in this world...

Two men came out of a house on Hægdehaugen. One was the son of the house, Fredrik Ihlen, dressed in a light gray summer suit with a silk hat and cane. The other was his friend from his school days, the radical Endre Bondesen. They paused for a moment and looked up to the windows on the second floor where a young girl with reddish hair stood waving. Ihlen called up to his sister:

"Goodbye, Charlotte."

The men waved back and walked on.

Bondesen wore a black, tight-fitting tweed suit, a silk cap, and a woolen shirt with laces across the front. It was obvious that he was a sportsman. He carried no cane.

"You do have your manuscript, don't you?" he asked.

And Ihlen replied that he had the manuscript.

"Ah, when the weather is like this, with this blue sky! And what must it be like over Sankt Hanshaugen, over the countryside, with an even bluer sky and a rustle in the trees! When I grow old I want to be a farmer."

Endre Bondesen was a law student. He was of average height and twenty years old, with a fine moustache and thin, neat hair under his hat. His complexion was pale, very pale, but his swaying gait and swinging arms showed how good-looking he was. Although he was not strong, he was agile and tough. He seldom studied anymore. Instead, he idled away his time, rode his bicycle, and was a radical. Financially, he was reasonably well off. Every month he received money from home, from his father, a landowner in Bergen, who did not look too closely at the amounts he sent. Endre did not spend much, but still he needed extra money every now and then, and he often thought of ways to get his father to give him a little more than his regular monthly allowance. For example, he had once written home that he was about to begin studying Roman law, and Roman law could only be studied in Rome, and so he asked for a small sum for the journey. And his father sent the money.

Ihlen was the same age as Bondesen, but a little thinner. He was also a little taller, with no beard, and with long, pale hands and narrow feet. His forehead wrinkled now and then above his nose.

In the street they met an acquaintance, and Bondesen said: "If only he knew what we were doing!"

He was in an excellent mood. Had he not finally, after three years, converted his friend the aristocrat? It was a proud day for him, and he had expressly given up a bicycle trip with his friends to Ejdsvold on the occasion. Charlotte had also sat and looked him straight in the face when, after twenty attempts, he eventually convinced her brother with his best arguments. Who knows, perhaps he had touched her a little too!

"Listen, you have the manuscript, haven't you?" he asked a second time. "You didn't leave it on the table, did you?"

Ihlen patted his breast pocket and again replied that he had it.

"Anyway, it wouldn't be like me to leave it lying on the table," he said. "And besides, it is hardly reasonable to think that he will accept it."

"He'll take it, he'll take it!" answered Bondesen. "Lynge will accept it at once. You don't know Editor Lynge. There are not many people in this country whom I admire as much him. Ever since I was a youngster and lived at home, he has taught me a great deal, and I am filled with gratitude whenever I see him on the street. It's a strange feeling. Have you ever known such a talent? Three or four lines in his newspaper say as much as a full column in other papers.

Knut Hamsun

§

Editor Lynge

(Redaktør Lynge)

Translated by Rick Schober

Tough Poets Press
Arlington, Massachusetts

Editor Lynge by Knut Hamsun (1893)
Original title: *Redaktør Lynge*

Translation copyright © 2023 by Rick Schober

Back cover photo: Knut Hamsun, circa 1903
Source: National Library of Norway

ISBN 979-8-218-26987-6

Tough Poets Press
Arlington, Massachusetts 02476
U.S.A.

www.toughpoets.com

Editor Lynge

He strikes in a petty way, yes, he does, but that's the way it is, for better or worse. Did you see his short note to the Ministry in the last edition? The first six lines were so mild, so peaceful, without any evil in mind, and then the seventh, a single line, a single line, a line that ended it all and left a lovely bloody whiplash. Yes, he has it! ... When you meet him, say such and such, you have written more than this, you have sent some of it abroad, and you have more in your head. And with that you present the manuscript. If only I had had something to bring to him, too! But if I should get something, I mean later on, maybe sometime next year, you must do me the favor of taking it to him. Yes, you must. I can't bring myself to do it, I know, for he has had such a strong influence on me."

"You talk as if I were a permanent employee of the *Gazette*."

"There is a big difference between you and me. You have an old, well-known name, for not everyone is called Ihlen. And besides, you write scholarly papers."

"What are you talking about?" cried Ihlen, wiping his face. "I can't just boldly burst into his office!"

"No, you are right! No, you must approach him calmly. Then I'll wait for you downstairs until you come out again. The Bear Højbro doesn't read the *Gazette* anymore, he said. Well, that is in keeping with the man's education. He doesn't read anything, of course..."

"Yes, he reads a lot," says Ihlen.

"Does he? Does Højbro read a lot? Well, if you want to keep up and be a modern person, you have to read the *Gazette*, I think. Højbro laughed when I said that the *Gazette* was radical. It was pure posturing. I am a radical, and I say that the *Gazette* is too. Of course, it advertises the fact and brags about itself. Quite frankly, why not? Haven't they good reason to feel superior? Other newspapers imitate it, even if it is only by putting headlines over the articles. They must learn it from the *Gazette*. Is it not true? By the way, you can say what you like, but the *Gazette* is the only paper with any influence worth mentioning. Lynge has—I almost said literally—brought the Ministry to its knees, and he is the man to lift it up again as well. Admittedly, he is working against his best interests, but is it Lynge's fault? Is it not the Ministry that is betraying its own old principles? Down with that miserable institution! Lynge will see to it."

"Since you mention headlines, I'm thinking that maybe I should put a headline on my article."

"What is it called now?"

"Now it's just called: 'A little about our berry varieties.'"

"Well, let us go into the Grand and think of another headline."

But after the two went into the Grand and drank a glass of champagne each, Bondesen changed his mind. "A little about our berry varieties" was not a title suitable for the *Gazette*. It didn't stand out, it wasn't clear, and it was also too long for a headline. But it was a humble title for a debut work to put on the desk of a great editor. They would leave it to Lynge himself to write the headline. There was no one like him to make headlines exciting. "A little about our berry varieties" was good enough for the time being.

And the men went out into the street again.

When they came to the *Gazette*'s offices, they both involuntarily slowed their pace. Bondesen looked quite anxious. The name of the paper was written over the gate, across the front of the building. From inside the printing office came the clatter of rollers and wheels.

"You see," said Bondesen, "there are great things going on here!" He spoke quietly despite the noise.

"Well, God knows how it will turn out now!" said Ihlen, smiling. "But I really don't expect anything more than a 'no.'"

"You just go up and do as I have told you," encouraged his friend. "You have sent something to a foreign journal, and you have more in your head. Here's a little about berries, about our berry varieties . . . I'll wait for you here."

Ihlen entered the editor's anteroom. Two men were sitting there writing and cutting with scissors, and the commotion was so great that it seemed to him that there were at least five of them working. He asked for the editor, and with a wave of the hand from one of the writers he was shown to the editor's private door, which he opened.

There were several people present, even a couple of women. In the middle of the room, at a desk by the wall, sat the editor himself, Alexander Lynge, the great journalist whom the whole town knew. He was a man of forty, with a marked, lively face and bright youthful eyes. His fair hair was cut close to his head, and his beard was neatly trimmed. Both his clothing and his shoes were new. Altogether he looked amiable and charming. The two ladies smiled at something he said, while he himself sat opening telegrams, for which he wrote headlines, adding many words underneath. When he bent over the desk his double chin showed, and his waistcoat made fat wrinkles over his stomach.

He nodded to Ihlen without interrupting his work.

Ihlen looked around. Pictures and clippings hung on the walls. Newspapers and magazines were everywhere, on tables, on chairs, in the windows, on the floor. Manuals and encyclopedias were piled up on a shelf above the editor's head. And on his desk so many papers and manuscripts were strewn about that he could hardly move his arms. Every corner of the room was occupied by this man's business. This quantity of printed matter, this disorder everywhere, these deep piles of magazines and books, gave the impression of vigorous and endless work. There was never a moment's silence. The telephone rang incessantly. People came and went, the machines whizzed in the printing office, and the postman brought new heaps of letters and newspapers. It was as if this newspaper boss was about to be buried in a sea of work, as if a miniature world was pouring in on him and waiting for his decisions in all things.

And in the middle of this bustle he himself sat with supreme calmness and managed the paper, writing headlines, taking important telephone calls, making notes on loose scraps of paper, chatting with the waiting people, and now and then opening the door to ask a question or give an order to his subordinates in the outer office. Everything was like a game to him. He even occasionally told a joke that made the ladies laugh. A poor woman entered. Lynge knew her and knew her business. She was evidently in the habit of coming to him on certain days. He handed her a crown across the table, nodded, and started writing again. He had his nets out everywhere, and the sword of the *Gazette* flashed over everyone's head. An editor is a state power, and Lynge's power was greater than anyone else's. He looked at the clock, got up and called out to his secretary:

"Has the Ministry not sent us any explanation yet?"

"No, they haven't."

Calmly, Lynge sat down again. He knew that the Ministry must agree to give him the explanation he had demanded, or else he would give it another shock, perhaps a blow to the head.

"God, how hard you are on the poor ministers!" said one of the ladies. "You are killing them."

But Lynge answered gravely and warmly:

"So it goes with every sworn soul in Norway!"

On his left, by the window, sat a person of great importance to the editor of the *Gazette*, a lean, gray-haired gentleman with glasses and a wig, Mr. Ole Brede. This man, a journalist without employment and who never wrote anything, was Lynge's friend and inseparable companion. Malicious tongues had given him the nickname Leporello* because he was always at Lynge's side. He did not write

---

*Translator's note: In printing, leporello is a type of binding for a leaflet in which the pages are printed on a long single sheet and folded in a zig-zag or accordion-like fashion. The term is derived from the name of the servant in Mozart's *Don Giovanni* who, at one point in the opera, unfolds a lengthy list of his master's romatic conquests.

anything for the paper. He had no other occupation than to occupy a chair and take up space. He never spoke without first being asked about something, and even then he searched for the fewest words. The man was a perfect mixture of stupidity and good nature, a man who was cold-blooded with indolence and amiable with need. The editor teased him by calling him "the poet," and Leporello smiled at this as if it were none of his business. When the two ladies got up to leave, the editor also rose, but Leporello remained seated.

"Goodbye," said the editor, bowing with a smile. "Don't forget your package, Miss. Goodbye."

Finally he turned to Ihlen:

"Was there something you wanted?"

Ihlen stepped forward.

"I have an article about our berry varieties which I was wondering if you could use."

"About our...?"

"Berry varieties."

The editor took the manuscript and, glancing at it, said:

"Have you written anything before?"

"I have sent a short treatise on garbage to the *Letterstedt Journal*, and I have several other works in mind. But..."

Ihlen stopped.

"Garbage and berries are not very fashionable topics," said the editor.

"Yes," replied Ihlen.

"What is your name?"

"Ihlen, Fredrik Ihlen."

The editor was a little surprised to hear this old, respectable name. An Ihlen had come to the *Gazette*, at last! And he had the pleasant feeling that his power was about to assume new dimensions. He glanced at the young man. He was well dressed, and did not seem to be in a very bad way, but God knows, perhaps things were rather hard for him at home, perhaps he had written this just to get a few shillings. But why did he not go to one of the right-wing papers? When had one ever heard of an Ihlen coming to the *Gazette* before? Anyway, berries were a neutral subject. There were certainly no right-wing politics in it.

"You can leave the article where it is and I'll take alook at it," he said, picking up some new papers.

Ihlen realizeed that his meeting was over and said goodbye.

When he went down to the gate and told Bondesen how his business had been cut short, his friend demanded to know the whole conversation, the exact words. He wanted to know what it looked like up there, how many people there were, what Lynge had said to everybody.

"'Sworn souls,' eh? Now, isn't *that* an expression?" he asked excitedly. 'Sworn souls.' That's great, I'll make a note of it. Well, you see, he has already accepted your article. Why else do you think he would have asked you to leave it with him?"

The two friends started home in the best of spirits. On the way they met a couple of friends, and Bondesen decided to buy them all drinks at the Grand.

II

The widow Ihlen had a small house on Hægdehaugen. She lived with her son and two daughters on the money she earned in various ways, mostly by fine needlework. She also had a small pension. She was a kind and stingy woman who knew how to make do with her resources even when they were scarce, and she was happy from morning to night. Recently, she had been fortunate to find a permanent lodger for her corner room, a man who paid cash on the spot, which was a great source of comfort to her. Thank God, now the worst of her troubles were over! In the beginning, when her children were young and her son was at school, it was often hard to make ends meet, but now that time was over. Fredrik had graduated and her daughters had both been confirmed.

Mrs. Ihlen went hurriedly in and out of doors, tidying up, dusting, cooking, and using every spare moment she had to make a few stitches in her embroidery. An unusual uneasiness had also come over her that day. She knew that Fredrik was now making his first attempt to earn money after his examinations, and everything would depend on how he fared. If only Fredrik could provide for himself, the whole house would be in good order. She could not deny that everything in her rooms had begun to betray a certain hollow prosperity, with new embroideries over old woodwork and cracked and battered stoves and beds. But it would eventually get better with time, she was sure.

Fredrik had been out for an unusually long time. He had left the house around eleven o'clock with Bondesen, but had not yet returned, and the dinner was already prepared. It was six o'clock.

The lodger had already come into the room, and was sitting talking to the girls as usual. Yes, he was a pleasant lodger, this Mr. Højbro. He had been out all day on his own business, attending to his duties at the bank in the morning, visiting the libraries, wandering his own paths, and when he came home in the evenings he often sat down with the family with a book or some papers which he was studying. The widow conserved light and heat for when Mr. Højbro was in the parlor, and he was also a source of great amusement to her girls, to whom he taught a thing or two. Furthermore, there was now the matter of the bicycle which he had given Charlotte. She really could not ask for a better lodger, and she would do anything to keep him.

The daughters were busy at their respective tasks. Charlotte was tall and plump, with reddish hair and a high bosom, and her skin was uncommonly fair, with tiny red spots and a deep, velvety softness. She had already made a name for herself in sporting circles through her acquaintance with Endre Bondesen and because of her own fine bicycle riding. Her sister Sofie was two years older, but was less developed and quite inconspicuous. Incidentally, there was a story about this young lady that the whole town knew:

One dark evening a gentleman had been walking back and forth in front of the Sculpture Museum with the specific intention of seeking a lady's escort home. The gentleman was Ole Brede, Leporello, but he had his coat collar turned up so that no one would recognize him. He then met a young woman and greeted her, and she responded.

Was he allowed to follow?

Yes, he could.

And the woman took the man through streets and alleys to a friend's house.

She lived there, she said, and it was necessary to go up quietly.

So the man took off his shoes and tiptoed up the stairs.

They stopped on the third floor. The doorway was open, and

they stepped inside.

Suddenly the woman threw the sitting room door wide open, and shoved the gentleman in front of her. The room was lit by many candles and full of people.

Then the woman pointed to the poor man who stood there with his shoes in his hands, looking dazedly at the company, and said:

"This man has spoken to me in the street!"

Her friends cried out, "My God, has he really spoken to you in the street!" But when they had settled down a bit, they realized who they had before them, and one after another, in astonishment, exclaimed Leporello's name.

After this, the gentleman realized that the best thing he could do was to disappear, and so he did.

The lady he had picked up was Sofie Ihlen.

The kind of people Lynge, this left-wing editor, had to deal with! How would he handle this matter? Of course, he would have to keep the whole thing quiet!

The next day the affair was discreetly reported in the *Gazette* under the headline: "Brave Young Lady." She had done exceedingly well, the *Gazette* said. Hers was a deed to be imitated. May it "call all our young ladies to higher goals!"

Yes, to higher goals.

This little article at once had a far greater effect in the Ihlen household than all of Endre Bondesen's left-wing arguments put together. From that day on, Bondesen was no longer forbidden to bring the *Gazette* to the house. What an editor this Lynge was after all! No person was safe from this man of exceptional character. After all, he had even disowned his own Leporello as a result of this prank.

The two sisters continued with their sewing, while the mother wandered in and out, and Mr. Højbro sat and watched. He was a gentleman of thirty, with almost jet-black hair and beard, but with blue eyes, and those eyes would look at you in a strange, blurred way.

Now and then, in distraction, he raised one heavy shoulder, then the other. He had an impressive appearance and seemed somewhat foreign because of his dark complexion.

Leo Højbro was usually very quiet and modest. He would typically speak only a few words when necessary and then look down again into his book or start thinking about something else. But if he became excited about some topic, his eyes would light up and he could be quite eloquent. This man, by the way, had been a student twelve years ago, and would occasionally lend his friends a crown or two when they needed it. He was like that. He had been staying with the Ihlens for five months now.

The ladies were always very hard-working, he remarked.

Oh yes, one had to keep at it.

What was it they were making, if he dared ask?

A carpet. Wasn't it beautiful! It was going to the exhibition. And when it was finished, Mama had promised them that they would each have a reasonable reward. Charlotte wanted a short, simple sports dress.

"And Miss Sofie?"

"A bank book of ten crowns," replied Sofie.

Højbro went back to reading his book.

"A blue sports dress," Charlotte repeated, and Højbro looked up at her.

"Yes, what then?"

"No, nothing. But I think it would be nice to wear a new dress for once when I ride."

Højbro muttered something about there being too much emphasis placed on sports. Hardly any people were left except those who could ride on something.

So? Well, these were the times. It was progress. By the way, what would Mr. Højbro's ideal young woman be like? A lady who walked, just walked?

No, he did not know about that. But he had once been a tutor in a home in the country which he had always remembered ever since. There were no warm baths or other luxuries there, but the young ladies were lively and spirited, healthy and full of hearty laughter from morning to night. They might have struggled if they had been examined in learned subjects. He was pretty sure they did not know the five eras of the earth, or the eight phases of the moon. But, God preserve us, how their hearts beat and their eyes shone! Yes, how knowledgeable they were in the arts, the little ones! One evening their mother told them that she had once owned ring with a blue stone in it, which she had lost. The ring was a present and God knows whether it was genuine. Bolette, who was the elder daughter, said: "If you still had that ring now, mother, I would have gotten it, wouldn't I?" But before her mother could answer, her sister Thora leaned in close to her and said that she should have gotten it. Then the two sisters sulked and got into a very amusing argument as to who should have inherited the ring if it had not been lost. And it was not at all because they wanted to deprive each other of the ring, but because both wanted to be first in their mother's heart.

"Oh!" said Charlotte, in wonder. "Was it so terribly important that the two sisters began to quarrel?"

"My God, if only you could have seen it for yourself!" replied Højbro. "It is difficult to describe, it was so touching. The mother finally said to the two: 'Listen, why are you girls so angry with each other? Do Bolette and Thora disagree?' 'Angry? Us?' they both exclaimed, and jumped up to hug each other, so tightly in fact that they both fell over backwards onto the floor. No, they were not enemies. They laughed with joy."

After this, there was a pause in the conversation. Sofie's needle was working furiously. Suddenly she stuck it in place, threw her work on the table, and said:

"What a bunch of sissies in the country!"

Then she went out. And again there was a pause.

"Oh, by the way, it was very thoughtful of you to give me the bicycle, Højbro," said Charlotte.

"Ah, I hope I haven't offended you. If you didn't have a bicycle, I would give you one again if you wanted it. I hope you will believe me. You are something special. I find no fault with you whatever, of course. If only you knew how happy it makes me to see you riding and . . . and in here! It doesn't matter to me where you are."

"Hush! No, Højbro!"

Sofie came back in.

Højbro stared down at his book. Troubled thoughts ran through his mind. Had he really offended Charlotte, the one he least of all wanted to offend? And he had not even had time to ask her for forgiveness. Again and again the bicycle story came up, this unfortunate bicycle matter which had cost him so many anxious hours. Yes, it was true, he had given her the bicycle, and he had made this despicable move with open eyes. In a moment of weakness, he had offered to buy her a bicycle, and it made her so happy that he had to keep his promise. Unfortunately, he did not have the means for it himself, not all of it. He didn't have that kind of money just lying around. Well, in short, he borrowed it. He got the funds from the very bank in which he worked by taking out a loan with forged co-signer's names. No one discovered his scheme and no one caught him. The names were provided, the signatures were forged, and the money was paid out. Since then he had been paying the loan back bit by bit each month. Thank God, there was just a little over half of it left, and he would keep paying faithfully thereafter. Yes, and he would happily do this all again, too, for he had seen Charlotte's eyes shining with joy only once, and that was when she got the bicycle. And nobody, no, nobody would ever detect the slightest thing!

"I do hope Fredrik comes soon!" said Sofie.

"Fredrik has promised us theater tickets if he is feeling all right tonight," Charlotte informed them.

Højbro held his place in his book with a finger and looked up.

"So that's why you ladies are so impatient, ha ha. Yes, yes, you are certainly entitled to some pleasure."

"Do you go to the theater?"

"No, I don't."

"You don't? Don't you go to the theater?" Sofie also asked.

"Oh no, I don't."

"But why not?"

"Oh, mostly because it bores me. To me it is the most wretched spectacle of all. I am so tired of such childish foolishness that I could stand up in the middle of the theater and howl with boredom."

Sophie was not offended. A man of such poor education was to be pitied.

"Poor you!" she said.

"Yes, yes, poor me!" he said, smiling.

Finally, there were footsteps in the hall, and Fredrik and Bondesen entered. They had perhaps had a few glasses, and were a little excited. They filled the room with their good humor.

"Congratulate us!" Bondesen immediately shouted.

"No? Is it true? Did it really go well?"

"No, no," Fredrik replied. "We don't know anything about that. But he kept the manuscript."

"I tell you, ladies, that it is exactly the same as his accepting it. That is the custom. I, Endre Moohr Bondesen, say so. So there!"

Then Mrs. Ihlen came in, and questions and answers went back and forth. No, thank you, they whould have nothing to eat. They had already eaten at the Grand to celebrate the occasion. It was the least they could do. They had also brought a bottle with them. They would surely have a drink from that.

And Bondesen fetched the bottle from his coat pocket.

Højbro got up and wanted to disappear, but Mrs. Ihlen called him back. Everybody became lively. They drank, toasted, and talked loudly.

"What are you reading there?" Bondesen asked. "Political economics?"

"Yes, it's not much," Højbro replied quietly.

"I suppose you read quite a lot?"

"No, I don't. I don't read much. Not really."

"Well, you certainly don't read the *Gazette*. I don't understand why everyone does not read that paper. But you know, I have heard that those who are most insistent about saying that they don't read the *Gazette* read it the most. If I'm not mistaken, I read it in the paper itself. By God, they weren't referring to you, were they? No, that was not about you. But tell me, what do you really have against the *Gazette*?"

"I don't really have anything against the *Gazette* as it is. I just don't read it anymore. I've lost interest in it. It's a ridiculous paper, in my opinion."

"What do you know? But isn't it true that it is the leading politcal paper of the day? You think it has no influence? That it has no influence at all? Have you ever seen Lynge waver an inch?"

"No, I don't know anything about that," he said.

"You don't know. But you should know what you're talking about. Well, excuse me."

Bondesen was in an excellent frame of mind, and spoke loudly and with lively gestures. Nothing could stop him.

"Have you been cycling today, Miss?" he asked. "No? But you didn't ride your bicycle yesterday either, did you? One must keep up with it, especially with the wonderful equipment you have. You know what I've heard? That even the pianist Wolff must practice two hours a day to keep up his playing. It's the same with sports. One must practice it daily. And you, Ihlen, old comrade! It would do you good to get on the wheel yourself. After all, you have shown that you are good at other things today, too. Well, shouldn't we empty a glass in honor of Fredrik Ihlen's debut, the first fruits of his labor? Cheers!"

He then moved closer to Charlotte and spoke more quietly. She really had to get out of the house more, he said, or she too would end up studying political economics like Højbro. And when Charlotte told him that she was going to be getting a new blue dress, he was delighted, and told her that it would suit her well. He hoped that he might have the honor of accompanying her that day! He asked and she agreed. They talked alone together in hushed tones while the others passed the time around the room.

It was eleven o'clock before Bondesen rose to go home. Standing in the doorway he turned around and said:

"You must keep an eye out for your essay, Ihlen. It is as likely that you will see it as soon as tomorrow as any other day. It may already have gone to the printers."

III

But Ihlen's little article on berry varieties did not appear the next day, nor any of the following days. Week after week passed without anything being done about it. Most likely, it lay hidden, buried among the other stacks of paper on the editor's desk.

Lynge had other things on his mind besides berries. Along with the two or three little angry editorials against the Ministry that the *Gazette* published each day, it was also the first with news of all sorts. It was responsible for keeping the moral order in the town, to be the watchful guard on every corner so that nothing could go wrong in the darkness. The support the old left-wing *Northman* received was very modest. The *Gazette*'s poor competitor had little or no influence and probably deserved no more, as poorly as it was written. One could easily see the inferiority of the *Northman* in its approach: no attacks, no angry words at all. With great restraint, it expressed its modest opinions about things and left it at that. When the *Northman* quarreled with a man, the man could calmly say: "Go ahead, attack me. I don't care. I can't be bothered with the matter!" And if he happened to get hit hard, he might feel it a little, but surely it wasn't enough to blacken his eyes or make him stagger. Editor Lynge was able to laugh at all this incompetence.

It was far different with the *Gazette*! Lynge wrote with claws, with a pen that cut like teeth. His sentences became swords that never failed and that everyone feared. What power and what skill! And he certainly needed both. There were too many shady things going on everywhere in the town and in the country. Why, he had to bring out the truth! For instance, there was that scoundrel of a carpenter up on the hill, who was practicing medicine for money, and cheating gullible poor people out of their pennies. Had he the right to do so? Was it not also the duty of the authorities to take action against the Swedish vagrant Larsson, who built houses here and there but did not keep his own property in order? Lynge had gotten his information about him from Mandal, and he was never wrong.

With his prodigious ability to dig in everywhere and sniff in the narrowest cracks for something to put in his newspaper, Lynge always brought something interesting out into the light of day. He carried on the work of a great missionary, filled with the high calling of the press, stern, restlessly passionate in his indignation and in his faith. He spared no one and nothing in his zeal. For him no person was above reproach. On the occasion of the King having given fifty kroner to a poorhouse, the *Gazette* reported in a single line that the King had donated "over twenty kroner to Norway's poor." And when the *Northman* felt compelled to reduce its subscription price by half, the *Gazette* announced the news under the headline: "The Beginning of the End." No one failed to notice it.

But he also honored people according to their merit. He had the eyes of the town upon him as he walked through the streets to and from the editorial office.

How different it was for him back in the old days, long ago, when he was young and unknown, and hardly anybody would bother to greet him in the street! Those days were over, those cold, hard student years when it was necessary to force his way forward, and finally struggle to pass his examinations with fairly decent grades. He was a young and enthusiastic country boy, a fast learner, and a quick thinker in a pinch. He felt great powers within him, and he tossed about with many ideas. Many times, he hd offered himself for employment, was rejected, and fell asleep at night with clenched fists. But just wait, yes, wait, his time would come! And now he ruled a city and could overthrow a ministry. He had become a mighty man in the eyes of the world. He had a house and a cottage, an honorable wife who had not come to him empty-handed, and a newspaper that brought in thousands a year. His years of hardship and humiliation were over. He had no other memory left of it than the simple blue peasant letters which he had tattooed on his hands once back home in the village, and which never faded, no matter how much he had rubbed them over the years. And every time he wrote, every time he moved to do something, those blue, disfiguring marks were still visible. His hands remained those of a common man.

But shouldn't his hands be marked by his work? Was there anyone who did such heavy lifting as he did? Where were the politicians, where were the newspapers? He was the one who led the way and made the rules. The old, insipid *Northman* merely stood in his way, and ruined matters with its clumsiness and toothlessness. It did not deserve the designation of a modern newspaper. And yet it had subscribers. There were really people who read this lifeless rag. Poor people, poor people! And Lynge, in his quiet mind, compared the two liberal papers, his own and the other, and concluded that the *Northman* did not deserve to exist. But as long as it lived, it lived, and he would certainly never do his colleague any harm. It would die on its own, for it had already come to the beginning of the end. Besides, he had much more important things on his mind.

Alexander Lynge was by no means satisfied with the thousands he earned and the fame he possessed. Something greater and something different had long been brewing in his mind. True, he was already known by everyone, and praised and talked about and feared by many people, but so what? What prevented him from doing something more, from extending his influence into every home and every mind? Did he not have the head and strength for it? Lately, he had been having the suspicion that he was not quite as good as he used to be. There were times when he felt he was not at his best, and he could not understand it. But it was nothing to worry about. He had the same passion in his heart and the same sharp pen in his hand, and no one would find him out of tune or worn out. He would be able to spread his influence even further, fill the halls in town and country, and cause the roar of his name to reach the rooftops. Why not? He did not need the few thousand subscribers that the *Northman* had. He could create new subscribers himself through his own work and talent. He would be able to amass many golden shillings in this way and his name would be on everyone's lips, everyone's lips!

He already had a plan in place for this operation, and his head was reeling with the brilliant coup he was contemplating. He had been so unspeakably lucky one day. A farmer had come into his office accusing his parish priest of the most scandalous relationship with his daughter, a child, a schoolgirl, who had not yet reached the age of ten.

Lynge was shocked. A priest, a married priest, and a young child, still in the cradle as it were! Had there ever been such backwardness? Had an infant been born?

Yes, an infant had been born. And what was more, the farmer had caught them in the act, had accidentally happened upon them. It broke his heart to see this for the first time.

The first time? Had he witnessed it more than once?

The farmer shook his head in despair. Yes, sadly, he had seen it twice, in order to be really sure that it was so. And the second time he had even had a brought along a witness so that he could not be mistaken in any possible way. Now that he, only a simple man, had the proof of what he saw, it was his unpleasant duty to file a complaint against the priest.

And the other man, the witness, who was he?

Well, here were all the papers. There was both the statement and the name, and he could read it over himself.

Lynge trembled with delight at this treasure, this goldmine of misery that was now to be exposed. The papers shook in his hand. The truth against high and low, against anyone who stained the law and society! He was happy that no one had interfered. If the farmer had gone to the *Northman*'s editor, the latter, in his fat duplicity masquerading as righteousness, would have reported the matter to the police and ruined the whole thing. Fortunately, the farmer had a little cleverness of his own, and knew exactly whom to go to. What a sensation his denunciation would create, what an outcry from the camp of the clergy! And in the end, it would further establish the *Gazette*'s reputation as essentially the only paper in the country worth reading.

And Lynge promised the farmer that he would take care of the matter with every means at his disposal. The priest would lose his office and would not sit there a day longer after he had been thoroughly exposed.

But the farmer remained seated in his chair, and he did not seem to want to leave immediately. Lynge assured him once more that the matter would be taken care of in the best possible way, but the farmer looked at him and said that . . . hm . . . that maybe he should have . . . gone directly to the authorities with this complaint.

No, no, but that was not necessary. It would probably have been published anyway. It could not have fallen into better hands.

No, no. But . . . hm . . . then he probably hadn't brought this . . . news for nothing, perhaps?

For nothing? What did he mean? Did he want to be compensated for . . .

Yes, a small compensation, yes. You could call it that. For the journey was long and it cost money both on steamship and railroad.

Editor Lynge stared at the man. Was this Norwegian farmer, this sharecropper, willing to exploit his own daughter for money? His forehead bulged, and he was on the point of striking out with his fist and showing the man the door, but he thought better of it. The farmer had a nerve. He had even planned this little business, and he was quite capable of circumventing the *Gazette* and bringing his secret to the police. And if the *Gazette* brought out its exposé the following day, it would no longer be an exposé in its true unadulterated purity if the police had already received the report. There would be no bomb, no lightning from a clear sky.

Lynge considered.

"How much do you think you must have for the news about your daughter?" he asked. For Lynge was always willing to gamble.

The farmer demanded to be paid handsomely, a large sum, hundreds, and it was clear that he wanted not only to be reimbursed for his traveling expenses, but blood money for the secret itself.

Lynge's indignation at the rascal rose again. And again he restrained himself. For nothing in the world would he let this affair slip through his fingers. It had to be revealed by the *Gazette*, with all the noise and anger, but also admiration, roaring around it. He reconsidered the situation. The case was clear, everything was in order, the priest had been caught in the act, and no mistake was possible. The statements had been made, and the infant had even been registered. For further certainty, it was the girl's father himself who was the accuser.

Lynge made a counteroffer.

But the farmer shook his head. It so happened that he also . . . hm . . . had to share with the witness he had brought with him the second time. No . . . hm. . . . it turned out that he had to get the whole sum.

Lynge was so deeply disgusted with this perverse father that he added a hundred crowns to his counteroffer just to be rid of him at once. But the farmer, who understood that Lynge was in a bind, did not budge an inch from his original demand. For in addition to all the rest, there was also the fact that he . . . hm . . . unfortunately he would have to suffer in many ways in his village afterwards because he had such a child. It would not be so good for him. He also had obligations, debts, and, to put it bluntly, he could not consider himself really blameless for ... hm. ... for the news with less than what he had demanded.

Lynge conceded. With deep contempt for this vile soul, he paid him the money. He went to the cashier himself and demanded that it be paid from his personal account, so as not to reveal the least of what was going on.

Now Lynge sat in his office with even more papers and more irrefutable evidence in his hands. He had spent the three days since the farmer's visit for a preliminary examination. He sent Leporello, his faithful man, to the scene of the crime to sniff around, and Leporello had come back with confirmation of everything.

And now the bomb was about to explode ...

People came and went in the office, the door never stood still, and the editor was in a most excellent mood. In addition to his good fortune with the celebrated scandal, which filled him with great joy, he also had a meeting in the evening, and this meeting was far too important to him. He joked, dispatched articles and telegrams with a smile, and gave his orders in the other office with a cheerful voice. His life was good. In a few hours the great coup would be a matter of fact, and the town would be awakened in the morning by news of the great event. Leporello had succeeded so well with his investigations that Lynge wanted to reward him with a small bonus in addition to what he was regularly paid, so grateful was the editor for the man's excellent work.

"I thank you," he said, and held out his hand to Leporello. And as there were several others present, they said nothing more.

Incidentally, he had a new favor to ask of Leporello. He had that day received a notice from a poor washerwoman from Hammersborg, a request for financial help. Good God, she had even sent payment along with it, forty-five öre for a single insertion! Was it not touching? He was happy that this letter had accidentally come to him instead of to the dispatch office. Now the woman could get her pennies back. They might be leftists, but they were not bloodsuckers. The woman had simply misunderstood the *Gazette*'s submission policy. He would ask Leporello to bring her a banknote, some initial help, and then he would establish a fund for her benefit later. All possible support was certainly needed here.

And with these words, Lynge even persuaded a couple of strangers who were in the office to make a contribution on the spot. His eyes were almost misty at this. He felt a pure sympathy for the unfortunate woman in Hammersborg.

He did not go home immediately from the office that night. He had so many things to do. He had to be both here and there and neglect nothing, and that evening there was to be an important meeting of the Labor Society. He hand-delivered his article on the scandal to his secretary and told him where he was going. He left the office like a youth, like a forty-year-old boy, with a spring in his step and his hat slightly askew.

IV

The great hall of the Labor Society was packed, and the discussion was in full swing. A right-wing man had wandered up to the podium, and attempted to make his voice heard in the debate, but he was frequently interrupted by shouts of abuse.

When Lynge entered, he stopped by the door for a moment, and looked out over the assembly. He quickly found the person he was looking for and then began to make his way through the hall. He nodded now and then to the right and left. Everyone knew him and moved aside to make way for him. He stopped at the far wall and cordially greeted a young lady with fair hair and dark eyes. She moved quickly to a bench, and he sat down beside her. It was obvious that she was expecting him. The lady was Mrs. Dagny Hansen, née Kielland, who had come from one of the coastal towns, and had been staying in Christiania for the past year while her husband, Lieutenant Hansen, was away. Her long hair was tied up in a knot, and her clothes were very expensive.

"Good evening," she said. "You are late."

"Yes, I had so much to do," he replied. But then he was no longer able to keep silent about his big secret, and he continued: "But every now and then my hard work is rewarded. Just now I am about to take down one of the country's best-known priests. The shot will be fired tomorrow."

"Take him down? What priest?"

"Don't worry," said Lynge, laughing. "It's not your father." At this she smiled, revealing slightly faded teeth behind her red lips.

"But what has this priest done?"

"Well," he replied, "they are all grave sins, sins of wickedness, haha."

"My God, how awful!"

She closed her eyes and was silent. She was not at all cheered up by news of this scandal. On the contrary, she had been a little sad all day, and now she was even more so. Were it not for the fact that she was sitting in the midst of a large public assembly, and constantly hearing the buzzing voices of the speakers on the lectern interrupted by the applause of the audience, she might well have held up her hands in front of her face and wept. During the last year, Mrs. Dagny was never able to hear of a scandal of any kind without shuddering a little.

For she, too, had her story, a little irregularity in her life. There were no grevous sins in it. No, there was not a single blemish, she knew that for certain, but still it was sinful enough, oh so sinful. The affair had not ended with the tip of a hat and a decorous farewell. No, the madman had gone headlong into the sea and had ended his life without saying a word. He had simply left her with all the consequences, and the result was that she had left home as soon as she could and settled in Christiania. She had also had another previous affair. A poor young theologian had fallen so madly in love with her that . . . but it was too pathetic, really too ridiculous, and she did not care to give it a second thought. It was another matter with Nagel, to whom she had almost given herself up so completely. She recalled the last time they met. One more word, one more half-prayer on his part, and she would have defied the world and thrown herself into his arms. But he had not uttered this half-prayer. He had not dared to do it again, and it was her own fault for having rejected him so cruelly before. It was, of course, all her fault.

Ever since, Mrs. Dagny had carried this guilt around with her. No one knew what was troubling her, but often she would fuss and fidget and jabber worse than the worst, and then all at once become sullen and silent. That was her nature.

And now came this business with the priest. She sensed what it was all about, and it did not cheer her up. Things were always going to go wrong, there were always those who did not look after themselves. Why couldn't things work out well for people, so that they could be happy in life? Lynge saw at once that he had put her in a bad mood. He knew her well enough not to be mistaken, and so he said in a low voice:

"Would you like me to withdraw the article?"

She looked at him in astonishment. She had not imagined feeling sorry for the priest. It was not his story that first and foremost tormented her. She said:

"Do you mean what you say?"

"Of course!" he replied.

"But how can you ask me such a question? Is not the priest guilty?"

"Yes, he is. But for your sake, you know . . ."

"Ah," she said, laughing, "you are playing a joke on me!"

But his offer had nevertheless put her in a better mood. He was capable of doing what he said, and she thanked him sincerely.

"I just can't understand how you get to know everything and manage to spy on all these people. You are matchless, Lynge!"

This: "You are matchless, Lynge!" thrilled him to the heart and made him happy. It was, in fact, so rare to be immediately recognized, regardless of his merits, and he replied gratefully with:

"One must have one's anglers out. One can never sleep. The press is a state power."

And he himself smiled at his words.

The right-wing man had finished his speech, and the moderator shouted:

"Mr. Bondesen has the floor."

And the radical Endre Bondesen stood up in the middle of the hall and quickly worked his way up towards the lectern. He had been sitting next to the Ihlen sisters, taking notes, and it was his intention to counter the previous speaker, the right-wing man, to the best of his ability. As he himself was a radical and modern man, he wanted to show the man back to his place, to his hole, to the dark, reactionary party from which he came. Bondesen had stood on this platform before, and had several times spouted his views across the hall.

"Yes, ladies and gentlemen, what is the truth? I hope that I may have your interest now, even for a brief moment. Here are just a few things I have taken note of. Recently a man stood here—yes, he has sat down now, on his laurels (Laughter), and tried to convince us modern people that the Left would lead the country astray. Not true. It took the courage of desperation to make that kind of statement to Norway's largest political party. We are Liberals, we are Radicals, but we are not fools, not anarchists, not monsters. If the country has gone astray, it has happened since the government had so scandalously gone to the right, and it was the current administration that has done it (Applause). What is the Liberal Party's platform? Justice, general democratization, universal suffrage for adult men and women, fiscal austerity, simplification of the civil service, the establishment of arbitration courts, and so on. All humane measures, all timely ideas. Then you come and talk about the country being on the wrong track! One could call our programs radical—one would be justified in doing so—but I would reject any harsher accusation."

Here the right-wing man rose again and said:

"But it was precisely because of its radicalism that I believe the Left is leading the country astray!"

The moderator broke in:

"Mr. Bondesen has the floor."

And then a timid Liberal interrupted:

"We do not take Mr. Bondesen's explanation of the Liberal Party as a radical party at face value. Mr. Bondesen is a radical and speaks from his own point of view, not from the Left's."

Then the moderator shouted with a thunderous voice:

"It is Mr. Bondesen who has the floor now!"

Bondesen, the man from Bergen, did not mind standing alone in the room as the great radical. He had stood alone before, and at that moment he felt bold enough to resume speaking. And as he went back to his speech he made his voice stronger to show how little afraid he was:

"The right always saw misguidance and deviation in every progressive movement, decline and decay in every advance. It must be hard to lose the understanding of one's own time in this way. For these people who have slowed down, lagged behind, and lay dead in the water now, they had once belonged to their time, they had been in vogue even fifty years ago (Laughter). But now they have fallen out of step with the present time, the democratic age of freedom. One should not condemn them too strongly because of this. One should feel pity for these few who were thus left behind when the rest of the world moved forward. Perhaps these few provided us all some indirect benefit. By their resistance they caused the rest of us to redouble our efforts in the service of progress (Applause). But we should never allow them to try to divert us from the path to liberty. They should be met at every point, beaten off the field in every debate. It should become clear to everyone, everyone, that the Right was a group of people who were doomed to be dragged along by the Left into victory, to lag behind and make themselves burdensome according to the laws and regulations of dead weight. And that the Left were the guardians of progress and the workers for change."

Bondesen was applauded every now and then for, in spite of his great radicalism, he made his points very well. The Ihlen sisters were overcome. They sat motionless and could not understand how there was so much in this friend of theirs, whom they knew never studied anything and never did any work. But what a mind, what talent!

Everything he said, his thoughts and his words, were easily comprehensible and touched everybody, durable left-wing truths gleaned from Parliament, from discussion meetings, and from newspapers. He spoke with forceful gestures, with a voice trembling with faith and enthusiasm, and it was a joy to hear this youth, a pure delight to listen to this radical soul who spoke so boldly. This is how all the youth in old Norway should be!

Bondesen was still leafing through his notes and had a few more words to say. He twirled his handsome moustache thoughtfully and pondered for a long time. How it must have strained him to deliver such a long speech on his feet! His esteemed opponent had taken the opportunity to rail against the government's hypocrisy, for which he should be thanked. On this score, they were in complete agreement, for it was far from him to want to defend a government that he wanted to overthrow with all his might. But he wanted to ask his honored opponent: what did the Left have to do with the government's hypocrisy? It was clear that the Left no longer recognized the present government as left-wing, especially not its leader, a man whose once great talents had faded. The government had failed, sold out or fallen asleep (Applause). And shouldn't there be an end to this talk of the Left's responsibility for the government's ineptitude? It was the Left that worked with all its might to overthrow the government, and the day would never come when the Left ceased to do so, for this so-called Left government had violated the principles of progress and democracy too flagrantly for too long. And it was the speaker's final word to the assembly that they should rise up, rise up against this handful of deceitful souls in the Norwegian nation and topple them from their thrones by all legal means.

Bondesen descended from the lectern to strong and prolonged applause. Charlotte and Sofie had never in their lives had thought that he could be so eloquent. How wonderful he sounded! Charlotte's nostrils flared and she breathed heavily as she followed him with her eyes. When he had come up to her, she nodded towards him, smiling, and Bondesen smiled back. He had been speaking for about a quarter of an hour, and was rather overheated. He wiped his forehead several times with his handkerchief.

Again the moderator's voice was heard:

"Mr. Carlsen has the floor."

Mr. Carlsen rose and declined the floor. He didn't want to say anything with regards to the Left as radicals, as this had already been done by someone else, and as Mr. Bondesen at the end of his excellent speech had said nothing more than what the Left in general would agree to, he had nothing further to add other than a thank you to Mr. Bondesen.

And Mr. Carlsen sat down.

"Mr. Høj ... Mr. Høj ..."

"It is presumably I who have the floor?" said a man, and stood up just below the podium. "Højbro," he added.

Bondesen knew all too well why Leo Højbro, the Bear, wanted to speak. He had been sitting right in front of the lectern and laughed all through Bondesen's presentation. He wanted to take revenge on him because he had been successful. He wanted to shine, to outdo him in Charlotte's presence. Yes, he knew it. The little applause Bondesen had received had not escaped Højbro's notice.

Højbro was not known to anybody. The moderator could not even pronounce his name, and when this new man stood up, the audience began to grow impatient. The moderator then took out his watch and announced that, from then on, each each speaker would be given only ten minutes, at which the assembly applauded.

Mrs. Dagny, who had been silent for a long time, whispered to Lynge:

"God, how dark that man is! See how his hair glistens!"

"I don't know him," replied Lynge indifferently.

Højbro began to speak from the place where he stood without

mounting the lectern. His voice was deep and gravelly, and his words came slowly. It was often difficult to understand what he meant, so ineffectually did he express himself, and he excused himself on the grounds that he was not accustomed to making speeches in public.

It had not been necessary to limit the time on his account. He might not even need ten minutes. All he had on his mind was a plea to all good people for mercy for the unhappy individuals who did not belong to any party, the homeless souls, the radicals, whom neither the Right nor the Left could reach. There were as many minds as there were heads. There were those who believed in left-wing politics and the Republic, and held this to be the most radical in the world, while others could not. There were those who believed in the most radical thing in the world, while others might have thought these questions through and already dismissed them many a year ago. The human soul could hardly be expressed in whole numbers. It consisted of nuances, of contradictions, of hundreds of fractions, and the more modern a soul was, the greater the complexity of nuances it possessed. But such a composite soul could hardly find a permanent place within the parties. What the parties taught and believed, these souls had long since outlived. They were radicals who, in the course of their development, had added to the quantum of fixed party consciousness they once had. They were rudderless comets who went their own way after abandoning everyone else's. And these were the ones he would pray for. As a rule, they were men of will, strong men. They had one goal: happiness, the greatest possible happiness, and they had one means: honesty, absolute incorruptibility, contempt for personal advantage. They fought life and death for their faith, they broke their backs for it, and they did not believe in fixed political principles. Therefore, they could not be party men, but they believed in the nobility of the heart. Their words could be heavy and harsh, and their weapons terribly dangerous. Why not? But they were pure in heart, and that was what mattered. He felt the lack of heart in the political parties, and that was why he wanted to offer a little warning to the Left, which was, after all, the party closest to him, that it should not depend too heavily on people without heart, but should take heed, look around, choose...

This was the essense of all his stammering. The assembly was more than generous when they did not shout him down. Never had a worse lecture been delivered in this hall, where so many poor fellows had stood up and spoken. He was awkward, stood stiff and uncomfortable as a mountain, took long pauses during which he muttered to himself and moved his lips, stuttered, and delivered a speech that was a jumble of confusion and repetition. No one understood him. And yet he really seemed compelled to say these words, to utter this poor warning that was on his mind. You could see that he had put his whole heart and soul into every muddled sentence, and even into the pauses.

Bondesen, who at first was sympathetic to him because he was doing so poorly, had finally become very impatient. In Højbro's broken words, he had sensed a few subtle remarks against him, and he was offended, and rightly so. He was deeply insulted and shouted:

"Get to the point! To the point, man!"

And the assembly joined in by also shouting: "To the point!"

It seemed to take no more than this interruption, this little opposition, to set Leo Højbro on fire. His ears pricked up. He knew this Bergen voice and knew where it came from, and smiling at the hostility he had aroused, he blurted out in his deep voice a few sentences that came like flashes, like sparks:

First, he made a little remark about Mr. Bondesen as a radical. Mr. Bondesen's radicalism was indeed very extreme, but he wanted to defend Mr. Bondesen against the assembly's overevaluation of his radicalism. One should not be afraid of him, for if Mr. Bondesen one day thought of offering his radicalism to other radicals, they would answer him: "I seem to remember that I dabbled with that once in my life, a very long time ago. It at about the same time I was first confirmed..."

Bondesen was not able to keep still any longer. He sprang up and shouted:

"That man... I know that man there, the rudderless comet. I don't know whether he can speak at all on political matters. He is as ignorant of Norwegian politics as a child. He doesn't even read the *Gazette* (Laughter). He says that the *Gazette* bores him, that he has lost interest in it (More laughter)."

Højbro smiled wryly and continued: "It would then be permissible for me to nitpick a little at another statement that had been made here tonight..."

But then the moderator intervened:

"Your time is up."

Højbro looked up to the podium behind him and said, pleadingly:

"Just five minutes more! Otherwise, my whole speech will be meaningless. Only two minutes more!"

But the moderator insisted that his decision with regard to the time limit be respected, and Højbro had to sit down.

"What a pity!" said Mrs. Dagny. "He had just begun."

She was perhaps the only one in the room who had paid attention, even though Højbro spoke so poorly. There was something about this man that made an impression on her: the sound of his voice, his strange opinions, the image of the rudderless comet. It was as if a faint echo of Johan Nagel's voice and image had floated past her. She shrugged her shoulders, however, and yawned. When, a little later, the room began to grow restless, and there were loud shouts for a vote, she said:

"Shall we not go? Will you be so kind as to take me home?"

Lynge got up at once and helped her put on her coat. It was a pleasure to him. He could not ask for anything better! And he told jokes that made her laugh as they went down the stairs and out into the street.

"Should I not write a story about him, this rudderless comet, and poke a little fun at him?"

"What? Oh no," she said. "Let him alone. Now, what really happened with that priest? Tell me, what has he done?"

But Lynge didn't say anything but a few words about the matter, and he kept all the rest to himself. Meanwhile, they had reached the town square, where they got into a cab and drove out along the Drammensvejen in the bright illumination of the streetlights.

V

For several days Cristiania talked of nothing but the great scandal. The morning when the bomb was dropped, it was as if the very foundations of the city were crumbling. When this mighty priest whose name was known all over the country was now beaten to the ground, then anyone, one's father, one's daughter, could be in danger of being taken down next. But Lynge was sure of his case. He paid no heed to threats and cries. His firmness could not be shaken. He brought up the case again and again in his newspaper, repeated his accusations in even more serious words, and when the initial sensation was over he made sure to keep the story alive with little additions, little forgotten bits. He exploited the case to the utmost, even put up a fight when interest began to wane, printed furious, anonymous letters he had received from the priest's supporters, and flooded the town with his revelations. The public simply surrendered. It was no use trying to ignore this editor. Everyone, even his bitter opponents, had to take a knee and admit that he was a devil of a fellow.

And Lynge triumphed for the first time in a big way. With this one coup he had gathered quite a few new subscribers. People whose lives had been fairly faultless read his paper for the sake of amusement and curiosity, to keep up with the scandals, and the poor wretches who had some secret sin on their consciences devoured the *Gazette* feverishly, their hearts pounding, full of fear that it would soon be their turn to be revealed.

It was then a matter of keeping the momentum going. He was not one to rest on his laurels. This priest's story was in reality only the first big strike. Lynge had not yet penetrated everywhere, into every house, into every heart. Yet the thought was always in his mind.

Frankly, he had hoped that the scandal would have created even more publicity and brought in more money. The newspaper's accounts did not show any real mass influx of new subscribers. They did not come in droves, and there were even a few simple souls who canceled their subscriptions precisely because of the scandal. How could one understand these people? Here he had brought them an utterly unprecedented piece of news, and they refused to read it! Well, at least for a time he had managed to be on everybody's lips. He had added to his already established reputation, and that in itself was worth a great deal of money. He felt far from exhausted and his spirits had been bolstered. And he still had to smile when he remembered how long the police and other authorities had hesitated to intervene, and how he had finally forced them so gracefully to act at his request. And the priest had been dismissed with a flourish.

Lynge was not at all cocky after his great victory. On the contrary, his good fortune had made him kinder and easier to deal with. He helped many poor people unselfishly, and even lightened the tone of his articles a little. Only the government he continued to treat as before, with all the ruthlessness he could put into his pen, defending his and the Left's old principles like a hero. No one could accuse him of being lukewarm.

He continued to receive more and more visits to his office than before. People came to show their esteem for him, to shake his hand. They invented trivial excuses to see him, greeted him on the telephone on the pretext that they had been mistakenly put in touch with him, apologized for the inconvenience, and forced him to engage in conversation. The President of the Odelsting,* who was a member of the Royal Commission, had arrived in the city and went to Lynge

---

*Translator's note: The lower chamber of the Norwegian Parliament.

with equal excitement. The honorable president, so respected as a politician, so powerful a man within the government's opposition, greeted the editor with true cordiality, as a friend and acquaintance, and Lynge gave him all the respect he deserved and listened to his every word.

Yes, the President said, the Royal Commission was too diverse in its composition to get any meaningful results from it. One side wanted one thing and the other another. If the government wanted to make amends for what it had done to the Left, it could have done so at the time the appointments to this commission were made.

Lynge replied:

"The government? Do you still expect anything from it?"

"No, unfortunately," the President said. "I wait and hope for nothing else than that it should fall."

And Lynge, who understood that this was a compliment to him, replied:

"We shall do our best!"

When the President turned to go, it struck Lynge how haggard and worn-out this faithful old fighter for the cause of the Left looked. His cotton sweater hung crookedly on his shoulders, and from the stripes down his thighs you could see that he had struck sulphur matches on his trousers. He stopped in the doorway and said that he was to hold a meeting, a long political lecture, at the Cristiania Public Library in a few days, and he would ask Lynge for assistance in getting it well publicized. By the way, he would also like to see Lynge himself down there, and hoped that he would show up.

Lynge replied that, yes, he would certainly do so. Of course, he would attend a matter of such importance as the Odelsting president's lecture. And they exchanged goodbyes.

With that, he turned to Leporello, who had come in, and asked:

"What is the news? What is the town talking about today?"

"The town is talking," replied Leporello, "about the *Northman*'s articles on the plight of our seamen. They have aroused tremendous attention. Wherever I have been today, people have been talking about these articles."

"Really? Really?"

And although they immediately went on to talk about something else, Leporello saw that the editor's thoughts were not with the conversation. He had something else on his mind. He was plotting something.

"It was an enjoyable evening last night at the Tivoli," said Leporello. "I had a very good time."

"So did I," replied Lynge, rising to his feet. He opened the door of the outer office and called to his secretary:

"Listen, write a piece about our seamen. Tell them that our previous articles on the plight of the seamen have attracted a great deal of attention, and even newspapers like *West Country Post* are now beginning to support us."

Although the secretary was accustomed to receiving many strange orders from the inner office without surprise, he stared at the editor.

"It is not we who have published those articles," he said. "It was the *Northman*."

Lynge frowned a little impatiently and replied:

"Nonsense! We must have had a notice, a mention somewhere. People don't bother to re-read old newspapers to see where this and that has appeared. Say that our preliminary mention of the plight of our seafarers has aroused unspeakable attention, and no wonder, and so on. You can have a full column. But hurry up so that it will be ready for tomorrow."

Then the editor closed his door and disappeared into his office.

Leporello did not get many words from him that day. Lynge was still very much occupied. He mumbled to himself, and answered "yes" or "no" to anything that was said to him.

Basically it was a hard life he led, and God knows that his hands must have been marked by such strenuous and often such unpleasant work as his. It was a matter of constantly pushing forward and keeping up, and what was there in return for it? His efforts were not at all appreciated. His ease ran away from him, and he thought the whole thing was not worth his hard work. Now the washerwoman from Hammersborg had come running in, complaining that she was not receiving her money. She thanked him for what he had already given her, but then began to cry, for once again she had nothing to live on, and her husband had no income as yet. This was an unpleasant scene for Lynge and it put him in a foul mood. He simply let the woman understand that he had a wife and children of his own to support, and besides, there was now a public relief office, and she would have to apply to it. Had he not already helped her once out of the goodness of his heart? God knows he had compassion for her, and had stretched himself further than he perhaps had a right to for his own sake. With regard to the fund he had promised to establish for her, he had completely forgotten about it. One could not keep track of everybody's concerns in one's head. Besides, he had not published her notice out of basic consideration for the woman, for had it been printed at the same time as the great revelation of the scandal, not a soul would have read it. It would have been skipped over like everything else in those days. He was going to do what he could, however, and publish it the next day.

No, there was no gratitude, no appreciation from anyone, least of all from educated people. He had worked like a slave all these years, had put forth his best efforts precisely for these members of the community. It was not worth his trouble. It was always repaid with simple scorn.

He had felt quite at home in Mrs. Dagny Hansen's rooms, where everything was fine and rich, where one dealt with educated people, and where one was appreciated as one ought to be. He had never come a step nearer to her than the first time he met her. No, she had flirted with him, she had beguiled his light heart, and laid her white hand on his arm, but he would never have imagined anything more than that, for no one, no one was more outgoing than this young lady from the coastal town. So he always had to return to his faded actress, whom few or no one cared to look at anymore. Yes, he reflected carefully, he did indeed have Mrs. L. from Bergen in the background, but this woman, who, on account of her obesity and white skin, was called "the Mountain Lady," was beginning to bore him unspeakably, and he was not the sort of man who could bear to be weighed down by anything. Had he failed to make an impression on Mrs. Dagny, he would still always enjoy looking upon her face, and would still be overwhelmed by the touch of her hand and the scent of her room. At every step he took in her apartment, he encountered something lovely and delicate, and his ears were filled with polite speech.

But how different it was in the environment where he spent most of his time! Politics and more politics, the government's hypocrisy, the royal commissions, the outcry of the poor, and no gratitude for his faithful work.

And so it was even with the President of the Odelsting, the greatest power in the party since the departure of his Excellency. A peasant from the fields, a man who had never had reason to learn common manners, a working man in cotton with sulphur stripes on the back of his trousers. But he needed to go no further than the farmer who sold the news of his daughter's dishonor for money, for the sound of clinking coins. Oh, it was incomprehensible! He really had to haggle with the knave just to keep him somewhat within the bounds of decency.

It was like that every step of the way. No education, no nobility, just simplicity, as far as he could see. Could he not make amends for this? He must at least be able to do something. And this was part of his great idea of conquering hearts, of subjugating the country. It was not enough that the masses read his newspaper and talked about him. He had higher aspirations. No one had yet perceived his goal.

"It is best that I go," said Leporello, as the editor was still occupied.

"No, wait a moment and we'll go together. I've finished."

And the same thing happened as so many times before as the editor walked with Leporello down the street. People greeted him, followed him, nudged each other in the side, and drew each other's attention to him. But what kind of people paid attention to him? Oh, average people, average people from all parts of the town, the whole world, the mob, and no one in particular. Nevertheless, his mood brightened, his good humor returned, and the two gentlemen strolled along the streets in quiet conversation. One was not allowed to stare. People must see that his eyes were open and his heart at work even now. He placed his hat a little more to one side.

A couple of bicyclists rode past, a gentleman and a lady. Lynge stopped. He had caught a glance from this young lady. He saw her voluptuous figure float by, and he asked:

"Did you see that lady? Who was it?"

And Leporello, who knew the whole town, and who also knew that she was Sofie Ihlen's sister, answered curtly:

"A Miss Ihlen. Charlotte Ihlen."

Poor Leporello had not forgotten how Sophie Ihlen had pulled him by the nose one evening and embarrassed him before a group of strangers with a shoe in each hand, and that is why he answered so sullenly. But Lynge wanted a more definite answer. A sudden recollection flashed through his mind, and he asked again:

"Ihlen?"

"Yes."

Lynge remembered that somewhere in his pile of papers there was an article submitted by an Ihlen. It was a young man in a gray suit. He suddenly remembered him clearly.

"Do you know if this Charlotte has a brother?" he asked.

"Yes!" replied Leporello. "She has a brother, Fredrik Ihlen. A little boring, a little ordinary, but otherwise an agreeable person."

And Lynge fell into thought again as he looked after the two riders. He recognized the gentleman. It was the radical peasant from the Labor Society meeting, but he had never seen the lady before. What a wonderful look she had cast upon him. It had almost been prayerful. It struck him right in the heart. And how elegantly she had rolled past, in a new blue dress that was as ravishingly short as it could be. For Lynge this was almost like a vision, a revelation. The young girl's gaze had instantly captivated him.

Suddenly he turned back. He told Leporello that he had forgotten something in the office and left.

Ihlen! This fine old name set his heart aflutter. And those eyes had struck him in passing. He could not resist them. Suppose he published this little article on berry varieties, authored by one of the best names in the country! What would people say? Really, a column in the *Gazette*! It might bring him as much recognition and as many subscribers as the scandal. People would take notice. No one would turn up their nose at the name of Ihlen. How he wanted to please the family! When he thought of her beseeching look . . .

Lynge went at once up to the editorial office and let himself in. He rummaged through the papers on his desk and found the article on the varieties of berries. After he had read through it, he began to search among the remaining papers and found some letters, which he also opened and examined. A little later he had arranged everything in his head, and he sat down to work.

And so Ihlen's article was to appear the following morning. It was high time. It could not wait a day longer. True, it was going to be drowned out by various other articles, but that could not be helped. Of course, the announcement of the Odelsting president's lecture and the washerwoman's appeal would have to be postponed. There was simply not room enough for everything.

VI

Lately, everything had begun to appear a bit gloomier than usual to Mrs. Ihlen. She could not understand what had happened to Charlotte during the last month. Her daughter had so completely lost her desire to work and all she could think of was getting into her blue dress and climbing on her bicycle. And this young man, Bondesen, continued to be spend time with her. That was well enough, for Charlotte seemed to be fond of him too, but my God, it was not good that he did not want to study more and make something of himself. His father may have been a well-to-do landowner and could afford to send him an allowance, but a son could not earn his living by such means.

Then there was another matter that worried the good Mrs. Ihlen quite a bit, and that was that her lodger. Hr. Højbro had come to her one day and announced his intention of giving up the corner room. It was the day after the meeting of the Labor Society, which the whole house had attended. She clapped her hands together and asked him why he wanted to leave them. Was there anything he did not like, anything in particular? She wanted to rectify it, to make it up to him. But when Højbro saw how unwilling she was to be rid of him, he reluctantly rescinded his resignation. He had nevertheless said that he wanted nothing more than to stay where he was, but that he would have preferred to live a little closer to the bank where he worked. Well, he stayed, but it was by no means certain that he would not one day repeat his desire to vacate his quarters in all seriousness, for he very seldom came into the parlor anymore, but remained in his room and was very silent.

All this made Mrs. Ihlen a little worried about the future.

She had expected so much from Fredrik when he finished his studies. She had a suspicion that he was no genius. He was a very ordinary young man of moderate talent. Even Sophie was far more clever in her way. But a man with a degree was by no means hopeless. He should be able to make some use of his learning, carve out a livelihood of some kind, and make a modest living for himself. Both Bondesen and the girls had placed so much hope in Fredrik's article, but Mrs. Ihlen was concerned that nothing would come of it. She even had the notion of sending Fredrik to America if he could not succeed here. In fact, there were many excellent people who traveled there. She knew several.

Then, all at once, matters took a different turn.

One day the *Gazette* published a special feature on Ihlen, first with Fredrik's article, and then with a story about Fredrik himself.

At the home of Widow Ihlen, they were overjoyed at the unexpected publication of his work. They had given up all hope of seeing his article printed. Fredrik himself had said, with a despondent shake of the head, that the article had likely been thrown into the wastepaper basket. His mother, who had no real understanding of the matter, had assumed that if it was not printed, it was probably no good, and so she had kept her hands working more diligently than ever.

Bondesen shouted as loud as he could at the news, hot with enthusiasm and proud to have been the cause of all this. True, they all had to wait a long time, and even Bondesen's faith in his friend's ability had secretly begun to weaken, but no sooner had the Ihlen number appeared than he threw himself on his bicycle and sprinted over at full speed. Well, what do you know! What had he been saying all the time? Not a day had he lost confidence in Lynge. Had it ever been known for Lynge to neglect his work? Was it not also he who first discovered the student's eye, the writer's eye, and determined his talent? Nothing escaped Lynge's attention. Anyone who said otherwise did not read the *Gazette*.

Bondesen was especially proud that it had turned out exactly as he had predicted with regard to the headline of Ihlen's article. It was no longer called: "A little about our berry varieties." Instead, there were three headlines in huge type, one above the other: "Berries. 2 Million Saved. A National Issue." See, these were titles that caught the eye, with which the great editor had dignified the article and made it worth reading. People could hardly resist an article when two million were involved! That was human nature, after all.

And next to this bold article on the front page, there appeared a double-column editorial piece about Ihlen himself: "Mr. Ihlen, by whom our newspaper today carries the sensational article on our berry varieties, had published a treatise on the subject of garbage in the last issue of *Letterstedt Journal*. It was a most excellent analysis of edible and poisonous garbage, odorous garbage, and garbage of the most delightful colors. If Mr. Ihlen had more of such things to bring to light, Norway could boast another famous scientist."

Ihlen himself read this entry with many misgivings, honest as he was and humble as he felt. But Bondesen swept all his doubts aside. What now, was he not satisfied? And he telegraphed to his father, the landowner, for a few extra crowns to celebrate the event.

They agreed that Ihlen should go down to Lynge and thank him personally for the honor, and Ihlen went. But in the town he happened to meet Højbro, who advised him against the whole thing. "Don't do it," Højbro had said. "God only knows whether you should do it, but I don't think so." But it was clear that, in spite of Højbro, it was the right thing to do. Lynge received him most graciously, inquired what he was now working on, and asked for more contributions. Then Ihlen received a very generous payment from the cashier for his article. He was very glad that he had gone to Lynge and thanked him.

Højbro always had his own strong opinions about things. He did not seem to be aware that people were starting to perceive him as very strange in so doing, indeed, not far from comical. Ever since the evening when he had attracted such unfortunate attention at the Labor Society meeting, Højbro had not been himself. He had become pale, silent, almost shy. Everyone in the Ihlen household did their best to soothe his misery, but Højbro smiled at these childish attempts, and in his stubbornness still made fun of the great leftist words about freedom and democratization and progress from the working-class community.

He met Charlotte one morning on the stairs. They both stopped quickly, and she blushed. Højbro asked with a wry smile:

"Well, why isn't the lady in her blue dress yet?" He looked at the clock, and added ironically: "It is half past eight."

Charlotte did not appreciate this. Perhaps, after all, she no longer liked the blue dress as much as everybody thought she did. But what was she to do? Bodensen dragged her along, the bicycle was polished, and the dress had to be put on. She was utterly silent and the corners of her mouth twitched a little.

He saw that he had offended her, and wanted to make amends, wanted to put it right. She was, after all, the loveliest thing on earth, and though he had been cruel, she stood there next to him by the railing without moving. It was more than he deserved.

"Forgive me!" he said. "I can't say that I didn't mean to poke fun at you, for I did. But I regret it."

"I think," she said, "that it must be the same to you whether I am in a blue or a gray dress."

"Yes, yes," he replied. And he grabbed his hat and wanted to leave.

"I only meant," she said again, "that it doesn't matter to you. After all, we hardly see you anymore."

He understood this courtesy with which she wanted to cover up the previous words. He answered just as cautiously, just as coolly:

"Well, I have a good deal of business to attend to for myself. I have been quite busy lately."

With that, he laughed a little, and bowed very deeply.

That same evening the whole family went to the theater on Fredrik's money, and Højbro sat alone at home. He stared at a book, but he did not read. Charlotte had turned pale. She was not unbecoming because of it. No, her fine face with its full lips had become even more delicate, more beautiful. There was nothing that could disfigure her. But there was perhaps still something that troubled her. Højbro also thought he had noticed a certain change in her relationship with Bondesen. They had grown closer. Once he had found them whispering together in the hall. Well, for him, at any rate, there was nothing more to be done. It had not been for his sake that she had blushed on the stairs this morning, as was evident from what she said to him later. What then? Clench your teeth, clench your hands, Leo Højbro! It was now just a matter for him to get his sad affair at the bank taken care of, and then settle down to his work and studies. He might have already been done with repaying the bank if Mrs. Ihlen had not come to him one day and asked to borrow some money, just until she received her pension for the half-year. Højbro had not been able to refuse her this favor. He regarded it as a sign of confidence on her part, and had been very glad of it. Perhaps he could manage the bank in other ways. He would try cutting his expenses a little, forego a meal every now and then. Besides, he had both a watch and an overcoat, of which he had little use. At any rate, the bank would have its money eventually.

Bondesen's father, the landowner in Bergen, had, after all, not sent as much money as his son had asked for at the time, but he had not completely cut him off. There was still enough for a few things, and Bondesen did not put a shilling aside, but spent it all.

"No, let me, let me open the bottles," he said, and took the pliers from Ihlen. "I am as practiced in physical activities as you are in intellectual ones, ha ha."

The mood was quite cheerful, and Mrs. Ihlen suggested that Højbro should also be induced to join in, but Højbro had perhaps already heard the popping of the corks, and was standing with his hat on, ready to go out when the lady approached him. Thank you very much, he could not. He had been invited to a card party in town this evening, and he was probably already late.

Bondesen shouted through two open doors:

"Come in, come in, man! I am not in the least offended because you spoke against me at the Labor Society meeting. I am in the habit of respecting every honest conviction."

Højbro gave a short, silent laugh, and went down the stairs.

"What a bear!" said Bondesen coolly. "He responds to a gesture of goodwill with a laugh."

A little later there was a knock at the front door. Ihlen went out himself to open it. No doubt it was just the postman, a "Here you are" and a "Thank you."

But it was not the postman. It was Editor Lynge.

Ihlen drew back in surprise, but Lynge smiled and said that he had only a very brief errand, a small favor he would ask as he passed by.

Surprised at the great honor, Ihlen called in at the open door:

"Mother, it is Mr. Editor Lynge. Won't you . . ."

The lady came at once and cordially asked the editor to come in. It was a pleasure, an honor . . .

And Lynge finally allowed himself to enter.

His prediction that the use of the Ihlen name would prove to be beneficial had been correct. People were amazed at the newly discovered genius, and at the news that a thorough exploitation of our berry varieties could make a man wealthy and enrich the country with two fat millions. Lynge again attracted attention by the impartiality and readiness with which he had also acknowledged a man from the camp of the opposite party. It was Lynge and Lynge alone. Who else would have wanted to do it? He was incomparable. Incidentally, there was also evidence of this man's impartiality from earlier times, as when he discovered the author Øjen, about whom he actually knew nothing except that he was a genius, but otherwise could easily have been the worst right-wing man in the world. And then there was the time when he disowned his own Leporello when he had been involved in a nocturnal adventure. Yes, Lynge was truly conscious of the great calling of the press! And he gained several subscribers by this maneuver.

Now his cleverness had again put him on to yet another idea, an excellent idea, and therefore he had come straight to the Ihlens without delay. True, for this reason he had had to miss the political meeting at the Christiania Public Library, where the President of the Odelsting was scheduled to speak, but one could not be in more than one place at a time.

He turned to Ihlen and immediately came to the matter at hand. It was something he had forgotten to mention when Mr. Ihlen last visited him in his office. He wanted to know if there was any reason why Mr. Ihlen's next treatise, on the cultivation of yeast, should not be published in the *Gazette* before it appeared elsewhere? Or whether he could not have the whole dissertation, or even parts of it, the main substance of the piece. It was primarily out of consideration for the bakeries that he made this request. And it was important to him to introduce improvements in the bread-making field, which it was within his power to accomplish.

But Ihlen had already submitted this article to a journal, a poor popular journal for all sorts of subjects, where he hoped to have it published. He told Lynge that it had indeed been sent.

Lynge responded:

"Then telegraph for it. We will of course pay for all the costs."

And Ihlen gratefully promised to do so.

The good Mrs. Ihlen could not contain herself any longer, and thanked Lynge with radiant eyes for all that he had done for Fredrik. He had pleased them all so much, and they owed him so much for it. It was all so unexpected and undeserved.

"Dear Madam, we simply have done our duty," replied Lynge.

"However, there was no one else but you who thought it was your duty."

"Yes," he said, "but the various other editors must have a more or less clear awareness of the task of the press."

"Yes, I suppose that is so. But we are so deeply grateful to you. We will not forget that it was from you that the first encouragement came."

And Lynge answered jokingly with a smile:

"I am pleased, ma'am, that this time it fell to me to show his talent a debt of gratitude. We Leftists are really human after all."

Then Endre Bondesen laughed out loud, and slapped his knee. Until now he had sat mute with admiration and had not moved from his chair. In fact, he was already half asleep when Lynge arrived, but that had quickly passed. Fortunately, they had not emptied all the bottles, and when they offered Lynge a glass, he accepted it at once and with thanks. He was in a good mood that evening.

He complimented Charlotte on her elegant bicycle-riding, which made her blush. Twice he leaned towards her to admire her handiwork. Otherwise he kept very much to himself, and talked mostly to the gentlemen—as if he had come for nothing else other than Ihlen's dissertation. All of his side glances at Charlotte were to mean nothing. How splendid she looked, so young and radiant! Her reddish hair shone like gold in the lamplight. He had never seen anything like it, and her eyebrows almost ran together over her nose. Even the little rose-colored spots on her face enchanted him. Youth stirred in the old gentleman, his boyish eyes sparkled, and he smiled with delight. How comfortable he was in this cozy family circle, where the room was full of young girls and admirers! The old, good name of the family greeted him everywhere, from the carvings on the old furniture, from the two or three family portraits on the walls, from every word these people said. They had been born with nobility, they had education in their blood. And Lynge did not notice how shabby and worn out everything had unfortunately become in Mrs. Ihlen's house. He no longer had an eye for the deficiencies, but settled down, like a man who had come to a party, and enjoyed the company. The panels in the walls were, of course, old, proud works of art, and the glasses from which they drank the cheap champagne were fine and polished. And how good it tasted to drink from cut glass!

Reluctantly, he got up to go, thanked them all for the great pleasure he had enjoyed, and went to the door.

"I hope you will bring me the treatise as soon as possible," he said to Ihlen. "Goodbye, then."

Lynge took the road further out of Hægdehaugen, far beyond his own home, to the outlying district, where the streets passed through empty fields and the houses were sparse. He searched for a Mr. Kongsvold, a fellow student from long ago who was employed in the Ministry of Justice. Lynge wanted to get a secret out of him when the time came. He had just had this inspired idea while he was at the Ihlens'. Even there, in the midst of those surroundings which so impressed him, face to face with the young lady by whom he had been so deeply affected, Lynge had kept his composure and let his quick mind work. He was not the great editor for nothing.

He found Kongsvold's modest home at last and entered.

"Don't be frightened," he said at once, and smiled, for he was still in a pleasant mood. He joked: "I have not come to interview you."

But Kongsvold, who felt honored by this visit, and who was at the same time very embarrassed, stood quite mute. He did not even remember that he had ever been on speaking terms with the editor. Lynge shook his hand in a friendly manner, and was his usual winning self. A little later the two acquaintances from their student days sat down at the table and began to talk.

Their destinies had been quite different. Lynge had been fortunate. He had become one of the country's best-known personalities, a powerful man who could bend necks and force his will with a single word. For twelve or fourteen years, Kongsvold had sat in the Ministry twiddling his thumbs. His salary was and remained miserable, and his coat sleeves were shiny from wear and tear. Promotion in the government offices was unreasonably slow.

Lynge asked:
"So how are you doing? Are you well?"
"Oh no," replied Kongsvold. "It's just one day at a time."
"Ah yes. I see."
Lynge looked around the room. It was by no means fitting for a royal minister's residence. A single large room was all that the occupant had. It was furnished with only two chairs, a desk, a cupboard, a bed, and a table. On one wall his overcoat was hung, gathering dust.

"It seems to me that you are advancing rather slowly, Kongsvold," said Lynge.
"Yes, unfortunately," he replied. "It could probably go faster."
"Well, it will probably get better from now on. The government will fall one day, and you will naturally have better prospects under a right-wing government. Yes, you are a right-wing man, aren't you?"
"Yes, I am."
"Yes, the government will fall. It must go. We will not accept the slightest scandal anymore."
"They haven't really had any scandals so far, however."
"No, that's where we are in agreement. We can forgive a left-wing government for stumbling, for allowing itself to be led by weakness

to make concessions to the opposing party. We forgive the honest sin of fragility. But here it is a question of personal dishonor, of breach of faith and laws, of direct damage to character, and we will never forgive that."

By the way, Lynge had come to ask a favor, a small gesture of goodwill. He hoped he had not come in vain.

It would be a pleasure for Kongsvold to do the editor a favor if he could.

"It concerns the appointments to the jury offices," said Lynge. "You will no doubt have to deal with that matter, and have it dispatched."

"I don't know."

"Well, there is no hurry. It is perhaps a long way off still. But I should like to have your agreement. If you are going to handle the recommendations, you could do me a favor."

"How?"

"In such a way that I would get the list of appointments from you at the same moment it is sent to Stockholm."

Kongsvold was silent.

"And if you are not the one who handles this matter, you can at least easily find out in the Ministry who is being recommended. I would like to be the first to bring this news, you understand. That's all I want."

Kongsvold still hesitated.

"I don't know whether I can do such a thing," he said. "But I suppose it couldn't be that dangerous."

Lynge began to laugh.

"Of course, you personally would not be mentioned to anyone. You are not afraid of my giving you away, are you, old friend? It is really only for the sake of my paper that I have come. These appointments are of great interest to the whole country, and I wanted the *Gazette* to be the first to divulge the secret. You would be doing me a simple favor, nothing else."

And now it came to Lynge's advantage that he had taken on Ihlen, a man with a long-established family name, as a contributor to his paper. He immediately mentioned Ihlen. Of course, he was Ihlen's political opposite, but that did not prevent him from recognizing his talent. In reality, he was not like so many other Leftists who stood blindly on their own. Yes, in principle he was dreadful, but my God, there were such people on the right too, and he had learned to appreciate many of them.

Kongsvold was pleased to see that an Ihlen had been recognized in the *Gazette*. He confessed this with a smile, almost embarrassed.

And Lynge assured Kongsvold that when he sought promotion, he would have the *Gazette*'s full support, not specifically in return for this friendly service, but in general, for the sake of justice. After all, the *Gazette* was not completely powerless, and hopefully would never become so.

So the two gentlemen agreed on this little affair.

Kongsvold found a bottle of sherry in the cupboard, and so Lynge did not leave until a couple of hours later. He rubbed his hands together. He had been active and lucky. His day had been well spent.

As he walked home he began to think about what was to appear in the *Gazette* the next morning. Yes, he had been in rare form when he wrote his little diatribe about the meeting in Trondhjem. And yes, it was a brilliant piece in a few choice words. All his old fierceness had come back to him when he wrote it. On the whole, it was a well-edited number he would be putting out in the morning, and he especially expected a great deal of interest from a four-column article about an Agent Jensen in Oslo who carried on a suspicious trade in cloth goods and would not allow his books to be examined by a man from the *Gazette*. One should not openly defy the modern press in its activities.

VII

The publication of Fredrik Ihlen's next dissertation was not long in coming. This small article on the cultivation of yeast was compiled from a couple of German journals, with conscientious and cautious conclusions after a number of tests, and characterized by Ihlen's honest confidence in the matter. This short piece, into which the author had put a great deal of time and effort, was given a prominent place in the *Gazette*. Ihlen himself could not understand why his work should be so honored. Now people began to talk about him, and people noticed him in the street. It was a pity that such a man did not get a government post, and he ought to have a laboratory, albeit a small one, a place where he could experiment on his own. He might be able to do something with it. He might be able to make important scientific discoveries. Well, for the time being, he had ended up with Lynge, and he did not want to leave there.

And Lynge was indefatigable in supporting him, in encouraging him and letting him try his hand. Nor was he hard pressed for income, for the two articles in the *Gazette* had enabled Fredrik to provide for his mother a little, and in addition he was able to purchase several valuable books. Lynge had taken the whole house of Ihlen under his patronage. Even old Mrs. Ihlen's needlework had received mention in the *Gazette*.

For some reason or other the *Gazette* also suddenly began to take an interest in sports. It carried long reports on racing, and the names of the victors were followed by exclamation marks, and were given such prominence that they couldn't be overlooked by anyone. The city's ten or twelve cyclists, all of whom could ride on anything, found in the *Gazette* the warmest friend who defended them against all abuse. They were given their own column in the paper, a formal sports bulletin that was always sprinkled with the names of the racers. This was a new area, a vast new territory that Lynge was taking under his wing. Every cycling shopkeeper became a devoted subscriber, and pale schoolgirls began to swing their arms and sway their shoulders on their trips up and down Slotsbakken. They looked exceedingly bold. One day the *Gazette* brought the rather interesting news that the Norwegian Colonel N. N.'s daughter had been seen in Copenhagen on the back of his team and harnessing four horses. What an exceptional youth! And the newspaper had already twice had the opportunity to publicly admire Charlotte Ihlen on her bicycle.

Lynge continued to report on various and interesting things each day. The morning mail inundated his office. There was no fire near or far, no murder, no mishap in the land without the *Gazette* receiving a lengthy telegram about it. Lynge's paper was becoming more and more indispensable in every household with an interest in the news.

He then had the idea of approaching his acquaintances in the artist community for contributions. These people, who could not write well and who even had some difficulty with spelling, filled up column after column with lively painterly jargon, and people enjoyed this diversion. Towards Christmas time, when the wheel sports were over and there was less and less to put in the paper, Lynge by a happy twist of fate got hold of a clergyman, a well-known right-wing man who had begun studying social issues and who had the courage to discuss these serious matters with his fellow men. Nothing could have pleased Lynge more than this man who, as a true rightist and clergyman, had begun to grapple with labor issues and tax reforms, and who immediately entrusted him with a number of articles for publication. What a stroke of pure luck it was that followed him!

How valuable the Reverend's articles were, despite how little thought might have gone into them. That was of little concern to Lynge. The important thing was that he had once again opened his columns to one of the country's most well-known names, and he wanted to show the world how highly he valued causes above persons. There was certainly more than one paper, both of the left and right, licking their chops after this distinguished clergyman who had come to the *Gazette*, and to no other, to discuss social issues.

The *Gazette* had to increase its size a little. The variety of material and the inclusion of American headlines overwhelmed it. People found a haven in the paper for small private matters. Businessmen modestly advertised in its columns and had their names printed on one occasion or another. A poor watchmaker who had become successful took it upon himself to provide dinner for thirty small children and brought the news to the *Gazette*, which gave the story a prominent position. And a professor had a short editorial note posted in the sad days after his six-year-old son had died. Lynge was present everywhere and had his representatives running from morning to night. And he had the satisfaction of seeing that the number of subscribers increased.

Editor Lynge would not admit to himself that he was doing these easy tricks with the newspaper to cover up its shortcomings. It could no longer be denied that it was beginning to lack its old fervor. His talent had reached its limit. He was the clever country boy with a good head and such strong instant indignation that he could compose an epigram with great ease, but that was as much as he could manage. He had to have others write anything that was to go over a column in length. He had gotten by with writing his six or seven lines for so many years, and he had put his stock of irony and bitterness into them. His strength began to wane, and more and more of his work was done in the outer office. But it would never occur to him to retire. His reputation was too deeply rooted in the general opinion, and he could still play his tricks with great skill. It was a matter of making up for the incipient deficiencies with new innovations, ever new surprises. There could never be too many revelations about delusional lay preachers in Western Norway or crooked agents in Oslo. When he felt that his critical skill, with which he had triumphed so brilliantly in many a battle, was on the decline, he changed tack, became objective, and suddenly began to criticize the tone of the press. How crude and undignified it was to discuss such a simple matter! The *Gazette* would not interfere in the business of other papers. It was too good for that, and it had more important tasks to devote its energies to. However, one should not transgress certain boundaries in the press, as educated people were wont to do in private discussion. The *Gazette* would simply not respond to attacks any more, and therefore it would be appreciated by all educated people. But people who had known Alexander Lynge a long time could not understand what his definition of educated was.

Above all, Lynge had to make the best use of Fredrik Ihlen. No publication could boast a finer name, with generals, bishops, and diocesan officials going back several generations. The young man had well handled the rather abstract subjects of berries and yeast cultivation, so what was stopping Lynge from giving him assignments with more topical issues? There were many subjects that could be included in a graduate's realm of professional knowledge. Lynge stopped him one day, just after Ihlen had presented him with a couple of columns on Norwegian wine and gin, and offered him a permanent position at the paper, with a salary of such and such.

Ihlen was stunned.

The offer was repeated.

Ihlen considered it.

Lynge then clarified that it was only to be regarded as temporary. There was no doubt that a grant or fellowship would come to Ihlen soon, so it was not an offer of a permanent contract, but of a temporary permanent position.

Ihlen found the offer most attractive and the salary unusually high, and so he accepted. The agreement was finalized.

Ihlen immediately got into a disagreement with Leo Højbro, who was known to interfere in other people's affairs. Højbro warned him against taking this step. "You will regret it," he said. "It is very risky." And he clasped Ihlen's hand and begged him to reconsider.

But Ihlen answered:

"I thank you for your interest in me. But here you must admit that it's a fine offer with a very high salary."

He wouldn't have been surprised if Højbro was so offended that he moved out of the Ihlen house. Thank God they were not entirely dependent on others anymore, and Endre Bondesen would probably want to rent the corner room if it became vacant.

As it turned out, Højbro was not thinking of moving at all, and he did not say another word about Ihlen's employment with the *Gazette*. He became even more withdrawn, and spent less and less time in the parlor. The girls sat almost alone all day. Højbro had also been less considerate lately. He had squandered a little of the goodwill everyone had shown him in the beginning, and one evening he had even made Sofie very angry. It was all about the most ridiculous trifle. They had inadvertently come to quarrel about marriage. Højbro could not understand why this dry, progressive woman with short hair should concern herself with such matters as marriage. He thought of her as a sort of male human being in a skirt, a creature of the third sex. He was in a wicked mood all the while and spoke to the young lady very sarcastically. Charlotte sat in her chair and listened, but said nothing. She squirmed now and then, as if the whole conversation tormented her. And yet Højbro felt that she was the only one who could have had a voice in the matter. Everything he said was for her sake, though he was bitterly annoyed at himself for having such thoughts.

The dispute had begun jokingly, with Sofie mentioning that she wanted to be married by the City Bailiff. It was practical, time-saving, money-saving, and without all the hypocrisy and humbug with God's name and all that.

Højbro replied that he would prefer to be married in the church. And not just in one of the domestic churches without art or beauty, not in such a carpentered room of God, but in a mighty house of God, a worldly structure with marble and mosaics and columns. And he would drive to the church in a carriage drawn by four black stallions, and each stallion would have white silk rosettes on its ears.

Well, wasn't that all very nice. And what was the bride-to-be going to be like?

Charlotte looked up. Yes, what should the bride be like? she also seemed to ask. And why did she look up just now? Her face was pure and fine, her expression as innocent as a child's.

He replied:

"The bride should be young and innocent." He thought it over and repeated once more, nodding: "Yes, young and innocent."

Charlotte turned bright red. She began busily to count the stitches in her work, and her fingers trembled. Then she set to work again, stitch by stitch, wondering if she might have made a mistake. God knows, but perhaps she had been sewing just right the whole time.

But now Miss Sofie became snide and laughed at him. Innocent? What did he mean by that? A bit stupid, wasn't he? A little ignorant?

"Yes, or a little less experienced than a girl with a child," replied Højbro roughly. "Call it what you will."

Sofie could contain herself no longer. She was outraged and called him out. She asked if such innocence was the highest male moral, and wanted to put him on the spot with further questions. Was he innocent in that way? Any man who had lived a little was not innocent! And though she was otherwise nothing if not good, she herself had dared to get a little sense of the facts of life, so . . .

But Højbro, for his part, understood that all this was just show on Miss Sofie's part. This person who was so lacking in human warmth, who had such weak temptations to overcome, whose passion was so dry and calm, liked to show herself to be experienced, complicit. He was silent. It was not for Sophie's sake that he had opened his mouth.

"But if she was never that innocent," Sophie repeated, "then . . ."

"Then I would not marry her, no," he interrupted.

Sophie chuckled. What was she laughing at? He shrugged his shoulders, and Sophie, who saw it, was at once embittered. She rose hastily and said:

"I leave the rest of your nonsense to Charlotte."

And Sofie stormed out of the room, looking quite pale and angry. Not a word was exchanged between Højbro and Charlotte. They both sat silent, and when Sofie returned they still had not spoken to each other.

Charlotte, who was as kind and warm as her sister was dry and tough, probably agreed with Højbro. He could sense it in her even though she did not look up at all. She returned to her sewing.

Lately, by the way, Charlotte had not been her usual self, not so cheerful, not quite the same playful young woman. Perhaps she had her own worries to deal with. She had begun to follow her brother down to the editorial office in the mornings. She had always been so graciously received by Lynge that she even looked forward to this diversion. Lynge's ability to entertain ladies was well known. He had many a joke up his sleeve and he did nothing to hide his great appreciation for high breasts and red lips. It was only in the company of women that he felt like a young man, so it was no use inviting Lynge to gatherings where there were no ladies present. Either he simply failed to show up, or he came, was bored for an hour, and disappeared again. No, without ladies there was no joy in his heart. One could just see how it was in the Journalists' Association: twenty men drinking and smoking, and not a skirt in the whole room. So Lynge stayed away month after month from the meetings of that organization, preferring to go elsewhere.

That's just the way he was. But no one could say that Editor Lynge was a womanizer. He didn't have that kind of disposition. He never lost his composure, nor did he do anything to further the matters of the heart. If he succeeded in his efforts with a woman, he was not dumbfounded. His heart was simply filled with a giggle at his good fortune, at his conquest. Tee-hee, you are mine, you are! And trembling with impatience to get somewhere with a woman, he presented the image of the happy country boy, who was himself half astonished at all the splendor he could now avail himself of. Was it not glorious that such marvels could happen to a man when he came to town?

The very first time Charlotte came down to his office, he abandoned all his work and devoted himself entirely to her. He had even made up an excuse to send Leporello out. He said frankly and straightforwardly that all this was done in her honor, and she blushed beautifully. Yes, how beautifully she blushed! The editor let her poke about in the manuscripts and periodicals as much as she liked, and meanwhile, he sat and watched her with great pleasure. How happy he was to have this girl right at his desk! But when she got up to leave, and he had given her one last warm glance from his boyish eyes, it turned out that Lynge had not been idle at all this time either. Even while his heart was throbbing with love, his mind was hard at work.

He called in Ihlen who was seated at the secretary's desk in the outer office. Ihlen got up quickly as there was a tone in the editor's voice that told him that something serious was going on.

And yet it wasn't all that important. The editor asked him, almost jokingly, about his political standpoint.

"Tell me, where do you actually stand on politics?" he asked with a smile.

Ihlen mumbled something about how he was unfortunately a

poor politician, and he hadn't had time to familiarize himself with the issues.

Whether Lynge meant it sincerely or whether he was showing a little spark of his usual cockiness, he said:

"No. Science has, of course, completely taken possession of you."

To this Ihlen made no reply.

"But you are a grown man. You must lean towards one party," Lynge added.

Ihlen confessed that he really had no knowledge as to what was going on.

"I have recently been influenced by Endre Bondesen," he said. "By Bondesen, the radical."

"Yes, yes, yes. Now, you should not regard this as pressure in any way, of course, but I have been thinking... What is your position on the Union question?*"

This was precisely Ihlen's weak point. He was a Unionist. Bondesen had not been able to shake his conviction on this issue. Why did Lynge want to know his standpoint on this particular question? Had he heard something? Would he perhaps dismiss him?

He answered proudly:

"I support the Union. I think it is best as it is, that we are best off as we are now."

Pause.

Ihlen believed that the conversation was over. He would excuse himself and return to his work.

"No, wait a minute!" said the editor. "Write some articles about the Union. Say honestly that you think it is best just as we have it

---

*Translator's note: From 1814 to 1905, Sweden and Norway were united (official name: the United Kingdoms of Sweden and Norway), sharing a common monarch and a common foreign policy, while maintaining separate constitutions, laws, legislatures, administrations, state churches, armed forces, and currencies.

now. Say also why you think it is best. Give your reasons. We are Leftists, but we respect all honest opinions. This diplomacy of ours also seems to be going very slowly. But of course, you don't want us to be part of Sweden!"

"No, I don't. Not any more than we already are."

"More than we are? We are not under Sweden. We are an independent nation, Article 1 of the Constitution. Now, you write these articles for the *Gazette*. You shall be given a free hand and be allowed to assert your own opinions. Then we'll see what comes of it."

And Ihlen left and shut the door behind him.

But just at that moment, when Lynge could well have used some peace and quiet to attend to all the work he had put aside during Charlotte's visit, one person after another came into his office and disturbed him. The washerwoman from Hammersborg had come again, for the third time. He had completely forgotten about her notice. What did people take the *Gazette* for? Was it merely paper in which one could wrap things, or was it a newspaper?

"I have looked at your appeal, and we cannot accept it," he said, and quickly busied himself with other pieces of paper on his desk.

The woman remained standing and did not say a word.

"We simply have no room for it," Lynge said.

She was certainly not the cleanest woman he had ever seen. This lady whose employment was washing for others obviously did not apply her skills to her own self. And why was she still standing there? He was used to having the final word. Nothing else was to be said when he was finished speaking.

"Then you won't be able to take it in, will you?" asked the woman quietly.

"No, I can't. Why don't you go to the *Evening Post* with it?"

She did not answer. She did not seem to understand.

Lynge reached into his pocket. If he had had any money with him he would have given her a crown, as pathetic as she looked. God knows he would have. He was not heartless, but he had grown tired of this woman's repeated visits. He no longer had any concern for her circumstances, and he had no money with him. He was, in fact, overjoyed when she finally left. What did one ever get in return for providing this sort of help? Not the slightest thing, only a "thank you" and then one was immediately forgotten.

An elderly gentleman entered. Lynge stood up and greeted him by name. It was the Norwegian politician and factory owner Birkeland, who was also a member of the Royal Commission. He looked pale and spoke in a broken, saddened voice.

"A heavy blow has struck us!" he said.

"A blow? What has happened? Has someone died?"

And Birkeland informed him that the President of the Odelsting had passed away. He had died suddenly that very morning, without any previous illness. A stroke put an end to him.

Lynge, too, was shaken, and he asked repeatedly: "The President of the Odelsting? Are you sure . . .? But such a tragedy! The greatest strength of the Left, the hope and support of the Party in all its difficulties!" Lynge was at that moment seized by a profound and immediate sadness. He realized fully well the significance of this sad event, that his party was deprived of its wisest and finest leader in the Parliament, the esteemed man whom the Right had no choice but to respect and honor. He said dully, with a slightly trembling voice:

"He simply cannot be replaced, Birkeland."

"No, we cannot replace him. I do not know what we can do."

Birkeland asked to use the telephone. He wanted to inform Ernst Sars of the news. He was not used to handling a telephone, and Lynge had to give him a few instructions, after which he sat down again.

Yes, it was the most painful loss that could befall the Liberal Party, just when so much was at stake. So many radical reforms had to be pushed through. How sad it was! Suddenly Lynge burst out laughing. He tried hard to hold back, but his face turned blood red and he broke into loud laughter.

Birkeland was finished. He turned from the phone and looked at him in astonishment. Lynge had found something to laugh about. His light soul had recovered, and he was still struggling to contain himself.

"Oh, it's nothing!" he said, shaking his head. "Have you ever closely observed a man talking on the telephone? He nods, tilts his head to one side, and looks attentive, just as if it were a human being and not a wooden box he was standing in front of. By the way, I do the same thing myself. Hahaha."

But Birkeland was in no mood for laughter. He forced a faint smile so as not to be rude, but his lips trembled. Then he brushed his gray hair from his forehead and found his hat. He still had some people to go to with the sad news, and it would probably be necessary to inform the government. Yes, he really did have a bleak view of the future.

And Lynge, who had become serious again, agreed.

When Birkeland was gone, Lynge immediately set to work preparing an extra page for the newspaper. By the time the evening papers were published he would already be ahead of them, and within an hour the town would know all about it. He wrote an excellent editorial, a little masterpiece, in which with a few lines he expressed his heartfelt thanks to the deceased for his faithful public service. Every word was full of feeling, of honest sorrow, and Lynge himself was satisfied with his work.

Then he went back to his pile of letters and manuscripts.

He stopped at a letter from a man he did not know, a youth who was living in a hovel in Tordenskjoldsgade and had nothing, absolutely nothing to live on. If he had some decent clothes, he would have presented himself in person to the editor. He was hoping to get some employment, a little translating or literary work. He had a major novel under his belt, but it wasn't finished and he couldn't get any money from it yet. There was something in this letter that touched Lynge. It sounded so credible and was so well written that Lynge's eyes misted over. He wanted to help this poor fellow, wanted to give him some work. And he put his ring on his left hand to remind himself of it.

When he left that afternoon, he stopped in front of his secretary and said, as he pulled on his gloves: "Do you have the minutes of the Odelsting president's lecture at the library?"

"Yes, it has just been sent up to the typesetting room."

"Have them send it down again, cut it up, and use four inches a day. We must do something to keep people amused. Here is a man who will come and talk through our newspaper for three weeks after he is dead."

And Lynge left, chuckling at his ingenuous idea.

VIII

Ihlen acted as a political writer, anonymously, on behalf of the editors. His articles on the Union generated much excitement, and Lynge had once again drawn the attention of the whole country to his newspaper. Christiania, in particular, seemed to be on the other end of the spectrum, and the *Northman*'s editor honestly asked everyone he met what it meant. The *Gazette*, which had never, as long as it had been in existence, shown any vacillation, which for twenty years had so bitterly hated the Union and its despicable fraternity, and which was rather closely associated with His Majesty; the *Gazette* whose editor had paid tribute to Gambetta, Castelar, and Ulyanov with heroic conviction; which had printed glorifying verses on the Polish Rising and the Brazilian coup d'état; which every day of its entire journalistic life had published articles, lines, and sentences in the true spirit of the Left and only in that spirit—the *Gazette* had changed! "Show us the man who dares to assume responsibility for the radical change in the Union that is being discussed," it printed. "We can safely say that such a man does not exist!"

These were powerful words.

Ihlen had done his deed with sincere and honest intent. His old love of the Right, his innate inheritance of conservative inclinations had naturally risen up in him during the preparation of these articles. It turned out to his surprise that Bondesen's influence had not

---

*Translator's note: Léon Gambetta (1838–1882), Emilio Castelar (1832–1899), and Aleksandr Ulyanov (1866–1887), left-wing political figures from France, Spain, and Russia, respectively.

penetrated very deeply into his heart after all. His articles, therefore, appeared as the product of a moderate right-wing man who had been given the opportunity to address a left-wing audience.

People could not understand this strange maneuver by the *Gazette*. The right-wing papers even began to quote it, to refer to it as a justification of their own ideology. One could now see that even the *Gazette* finally found the Left's policies too harsh. Even it no longer seemed to find it justifiable to continue the unscrupulous work of trampling down the most sacred interests of the Fatherland! But sensible people who understood Lynge knew in their heart of hearts that this was just another one of his jokes, a mere prank that was not to be taken literally. It was to be regarded as nothing more. No, Lynge was not to be trifled with. He was too sly for his enemies! Naturally, he had let this submitter—yes, submitter—have a little fun. Yes, these articles were simply submissions for which the newspaper itself had no responsibility. When Bondesen learned from Ihlen who the real author was, he was at first indignant that all his efforts to convert his friend had been so fruitless, but then he was happy to realize that the articles did not reflect the paper's true political stance. No one was going to deceive him into thinking that Ihlen had any influence whatsoever on the *Gazette*'s position. Surely Ihlen didn't believe that his and the newspaper's viewpoints on the Union were one and the same. He was indeed a scientist, he could handle the magnifying glass and find fungus in cheese, but he could not transform the *Gazette*'s twenty-year-old politics. And no one else believed it either.

Bondesen explained this to Mrs. Ihlen and the girls, and made no secret of the fact that he disagreed heart and soul with Fredrik's politics.

Sofie replied:

"Højbro said that he expected it, that he had expected this trick of the *Gazette*. He said it yesterday."

"Yes," said Bondesen, shrugging his shoulders, "apparently there is nothing that Højbro does not know and has not anticipated long in advance."

It was early in the morning. The girls sat in their dressing gowns and worked. The fire crackled and burned in the stove. Fredrik was not awake yet.

Bondesen continued:

"I met Højbro yesterday, too, but he said nothing to me. Instead, he goes to the ladies with the news."

"Well, why not go to the ladies just as well?" replied Sofie furiously.

Too many times she had put up with Bondesen's misogynistic remarks and she would no longer tolerate them. He was a radical, he spoke words of liberty, and he worked openly for women's suffrage, but deep down he carried the haughty conviction that a woman was inferior to him. Women were human beings, one half of humanity, but men were not human beings! Sophie was on the point of showing her claws.

Bondesen relented. He had merely said that Højbro had gone to the ladies with a bit of wisdom. He had communicated a fact, that was all. Højbro had not spoken a word to him. On the contrary, he had avoided him completely.

And it was true, Højbro had begun to avoid everyone on the street. He didn't even have an overcoat anymore, and his watch was also gone. He didn't want to force anyone to talk to a man without an overcoat on the street on a winter's day. He was not cold. God knows he kept the heat in him as he crept through the streets to and from the bank, shivering and with his eyes searching. But he didn't look good anymore. In fact, he looked terrible. He knew that himself. Well, now there were not so many months to go before spring, and perhaps he could get his overcoat back again before that. It was not impossible. And one thing was certain, he was not cold. He felt fine.

"Has Højbro gone to the office?" Bondesen asked.

"He is going now," replied Charlotte.

And Højbro's footsteps were heard in the hall. He was in the habit of leaving the house early so as not to meet anybody on the stairs.

Bondesen opened the door and called him in. Højbro answered that he had to go. But when Charlotte got up at once and waved to him, he came to the door and greeted her.

How long it had been since they had seen him! Why had he become such a stranger?

Højbro laughed. No, he had not become a stranger. He just had something he was working on, truly, something that was keeping him busy for the time being.

"Tell me," said Bondesen, "what is your opinion of the *Gazette*'s Union articles?"

He did not know.

"But you know who the author is, don't you?"

Yes, he had heard that.

"Perhaps you have not read the articles, you who do not read the *Gazette* at all?"

Yes, he had read these articles.

"Well, what do you know! But do you think that the *Gazette* itself shares the opinion of this submitter, this contributor?"

Again, he did not know this.

"But didn't you yourself say yesterday that you had expected this wavering on the part of the *Gazette*?"

Højbro remembered this and replied:

"Yes, I probably said something like that yesterday to Miss Sofie, but I may have misspoken. Of course, I did not anticipate anything at all from the *Gazette*. I am not all-knowing. I simply meant to say that I was not at all surprised by this maneuver on the part of the *Gazette*."

"Do you know Lynge very well?" asked Bondesen. "Is he a personal acquaintance of yours?"

Højbro made no reply to this. He was annoyed, and addressed a few words to the girls.

But Bondesen repeated his question, and glared at him.

"Would you really like to know?" replied Højbro. But all at once his face became red, and he continued: "You who are such a radical, who have your own party, how do you feel about the politics of the *Gazette*?"

"Well, I can't say that it has deprived me of my sleep . . ."

Højbro interrupted him hotly:

"No, that is precisely the advantage that you and yours have—let me repeat: you and yours—you are so very good at finding your bearings in such an imbalance that comes from 'other convictions.' You do not lose your heads, you do not blush with anger or shame. Instead, you walk right into the change and look around, and little by little you settle yourselves into it. Little by little, you embrace this new conviction which is just as genuine—and just as lasting—as the first. This is what it means to be modern."

How coarsely and badly said this was! Højbro himself felt that he had been rude, and was embarrassed. He felt everyone's eyes on him, and he lowered his head.

Bodenson lost his temper. He said, it was not "him" and "his" that were in question. It was Lynge that he had an issue with.

As always with Højbro, when he was met with hostility, he glowered, put his hands in his pockets, and began to pace back and forth. He had evidently quite forgotten that he was in Mrs. Ihlen's parlor.

"You would like to know my little opinion of Lynge?" he asked. "God knows why, but you seem to want to know it. I will tell you what I think in a few words. Lynge is one of us peasant students who has been wounded inwardly by being transferred to a foreign soil and environment. He is a little country bumpkin who wants to act like a man of liberty and a public servant, which he was not born to do. The man is without heart. His blood is false in him. To put it more precisely, he is a gifted rascal who will never grow up. That is my humble opinion."

Bondesen opened his eyes. His anger had left him. He stared at Højbro and said:

"But psychologically Lynge is certainly different, I mean psychologically..."

"Psychologically? The man is so far devoid of psychology! Say that he does all his deeds either out of a passion for the arts or out of petty calculations, or a combination of both. Say that he does everything out of a desire to be on the lips of every Christianian, out of an urge to be regarded as a damned great editor for his little piece of paper, out of a peasant-crazy craving for a few hundred crowns more profit a year. Then you have the whole man and his psychology!"

Bondesen recovered, and he thought the conversation was starting to get interesting. It was really becoming quite enjoyable to listen to Højbro. He said:

"But I don't understand why you have become so furious with Lynge. You don't belong to his party after all. You are a rudderless comet. What has he done to upset you? Isn't it the same to you whether the Left wins or goes to the dogs?"

"Well, here we come again to the remarkable thing about you and yours. You find it so difficult to understand how one can be hurt by finding oneself betrayed in one's ideal belief in a man or a cause, and betrayed by the mere words of a speculator, in this case an editor. I will tell you something: do you know that I have been happy with Lynge, that I have always admired Lynge? I have secretly written furious private letters to those who have scolded him in the newspapers. By God in heaven, I have been the warmest friend he has ever had. When I heard of a man, a high military officer, who had privately complained that the Right had not taken Lynge to court, because Lynge was allegedly a liar, I wrote to that officer, drove him back point by point, and called him an abuser of honor and a liar. And underneath I put my name and address. This was before I got to know a little of Lynge. Why am I angry with him? Believe me, I am not angry with him. He has become so insignificant to me that I no longer care to take his newspaper in my hand. I remember him simply because he exists and because he runs his little racket successfully. People think he publishes an amusing paper. Read it, study it, and see how this little empty man with no convictions, with no other courage than impudence, how this man who is driven solely by his desire to keep himself financially secure and to be talked about and debated by people in the street, see how he writes and what he writes about! He rubs his hands together at having a poor wretch taken down by one of his informers. He exposes the man with his chest heaving with rapture that no other paper has beaten him to the punch in sniffing out this sinner. What a glorious human pity to throw out to the public! His honored readers could not ask for a more superb misery. The fact of the matter is this: The man is corrupt, and he has no soul. When he can, in all honesty, manage a line, a trick, whereby he can get a few more crowns of subscription money, he is satisfied. He is filled with pleasure at such a trifle of a joke. He grins and gloats over the fact that he is the first to bring news of a fire in the Mjø region to a few thousand good people. When there is a public meeting in Drammen, he demands that the telegraph station remain opened at the public's expense until the meeting is over. And how much does this outrageous demand to keep the telegraph station open cost? As much as seventy-five øre for half an hour! But I do know that such a demand would not have been met if it had come from another paper, for example from the *Northman*. Lynge has corrupted people's ability to keep up their modesty. By his incessant bluster he has managed to dispel people's natural aversion to exorbitance. And afterwards he becomes ironic about his achievements, laughing and irresponsible, humorous and empty: 'The *Gazette* has interviewed a diver and a dirigible pilot. The *Gazette* is the best-informed magazine in the sea and in the air.'"

Højbro stopped for a moment, and Bondesen said:

"I shall not enter into a quarrel with you, for you value Lynge's work far too low. That is ridiculous. Is it of no importance that the *Gazette* found a priest guilty of criminal relations with a child?"

"Good God, how horrible to publish such a scandal just to get a few more subscribers. Yes, of course, absolutely, just for that reason! It should have been brought to the police, which would have been the only right thing to do."

"Well, the priest was dismissed, thank God. I look at the results. Agent Jensen in Oslo was conducting illegal traffic in clothes. The *Gazette* got wind of it, went to the man and demanded to see his books. The man refused, the *Gazette* published a couple of articles, and three weeks later Agent Jensen had to pack his bags and leave for America. Another result."

"Another example of Lynge's desire for a few more subscribers. This man acts as a conniving detective. He will enter the houses and hold interrogations and examinations. He says: 'Here you are, lay out your books!' I would, by God and his angels, take the little fellow by the tips of his shoes and throw him down the stairs if he ever came to me. And this even though I was never trafficking in illegal clothes . . .'"

"Well, beware, he may come one day."

"He shall be welcome. He is too poorly groomed to risk his shirt on a major offense. He never rides out farther than he thinks he can carry himself. He prefers the dark ways, the underhanded, the kiss in the corners, the handshake in secret, the swindle under the pretext of wanting to purify society. All men ought to see it."

The bell rang. Sofie went to answer it, and she returned with the latest issue of the *Gazette*. Bondesen pored over it with his usual interest.

But in this issue, Lynge had clearly and firmly raised a flag. An editorial article explained the newspaper's relationship to the sensational Union articles. Doubts had been expressed as to whether these articles were written by the editors themselves or had come from a submitter. To enlighten these honored doubters, Lynge had to announce that the articles were the *Gazette*'s own, that it was his own political standpoint they claimed, and that the newspaper alone was responsible for them. Period.

Bondesen read silently with his mouth open, a prey to conflicting emotions. How woefully wrong he had been. He threw the paper over to Højbro, and said not a word.

Højbro glanced at an article about a prankster in the marketplace who had been discovered by one of the *Gazette*'s people. She had been caught cheating the townspeople at cards for shots of spirits and cups of coffee. How she drew people in! How she played them for suckers! The article concluded that more schools and more public education were called for.

At last, he came to the editor's statement. He read it like the rest, without showing any surprise, and said when he had finished:

"Well, here you see for yourself."

"Yes," replied Bondesen, "I see it."

Pause.

Højbro got up to leave.

But Bondesen had an idea, a fine and shrewd thought.

"Are you absolutely sure that Lynge hasn't an ulterior motive in this?" he asked. "Can't you imagine the possibility of that man having a secret mission in mind? That by these maneuvers he will try to penetrate the Right, will be read by the Right, and then, little by little, sprinkle left-wing poison into the party?"

"In the first place," replied Højbro, "I hope for the Right's own sake that it does not have so wretched a conviction that it wavers because of the *Gazette*'s work. This party with its old education and skill should not be caught up in something so petty. But secondly, you are wrong about Lynge. What is he now suspected of, or what can he risk being suspected of? Of doing whatever he always does just to create fuss and noise and attract the curious subscribers. But the man would not tolerate such a suspicion being held against him for years if he did not deserve it. He is not big enough. If his main motive was to bring right-wing souls over to the Left, he would not be able to keep quiet about it. He would pour it out, divulge that secret too, tell it in big type on the front page. But perhaps he likes you and others to think him so magnificently opaque."

To this, Bondesen answered nothing. He shrugged his shoulders.

"Well, neither of us is going to change the appearance of the world," he finally said. "To be honest, when I read this statement by Lynge, and I see his reasoning, I have to admire him all the same. He is a devil of a fellow! Now his opponents within the Left, his competitors, probably thought they had him duped because of these Union articles. But he is still on top!"

"There are," replied Højbro, "only two kinds of people who always succeed in life and come out on top in all matters. These are, first, the honest of heart. They succeed. They are not always practical, but actually, in their innermost being, are on top. And then there are the morally compromised, the impudent ones barely within the bounds of the law, who have been deprived of the ability to feel scruples. They can do whatever they want to succeed."

Bondesen felt that these incessant responses to accusations were getting too personal, pushing him aside. Perhaps he had succumbed to this verbal abuse. He had not asserted himself sufficiently. And he spoke:

"Well, there's nothing more to talk about. One doesn't convert grown-up people with a few remarks. But be that as it may, when a man like Lynge changes his previously advocated policies, it is an invitation for each of us children, in comparison with him, to reconsider the matter. By the way, Lynge's motives have really amazed me. I can hardly believe that these simple things had never occurred to me before. They seem so clear to me now."

Højbro laughed loud and strong. "I had expected it!" he said.

"But mind you, I reserve the right to think these matters over once more for myself. I . . ."

"Yes, do it, do it! Hahaha. That is precisely—as I have said—the good thing about some people: that they can settle down so easily with beliefs that appear a little irregular. Such irregularity does not make them turn pale with emotion, does not deprive them of sleep and appetite. They step forward into the change, look around a little, and stay there. Ah yes!"

The girls had not spoken a word till now. For a moment Charlotte looked at the Bondesen, and then she too began to laugh, and said:

"Yes, that was exactly what Mr. Højbro said."

At once, Bondesen's face turned red, and he answered with a quivering voice:

"It is quite indifferent to me what Mr. Højbro said or did not say. I don't need you as a witness. This is a matter you know nothing about."

What arrogance! Charlotte bent her face deep down towards her work. A little later, when she looked up, she gazed steadily at Bodensen.

"What is it you want to say?" Bondesen asked, still agitated.

Højbro intervened with a stupid and insulting remark, which he later regretted:

"The lady is trying to make you aware that she is not on good terms with you."

Bodensen was confused for a moment. He said: "Oh, I beg

your pardon!" But then all at once anger stabbed him again, and he revealed a secret, which he ought to have kept, turning to Højbro and answering:

"By the way, I would like to point out to you that the Miss did not want to make me aware of anything. She and I are, in fact, courting."

Højbro had to let the matter drop. He turned pale, bowed, and begged their forgiveness. He looked at Charlotte. The look she had given Bondesen was one of great joy. How strange it was that she looked at him with such a radiant look.

Højbro did not understand it. Well, it was none of his business either! The two were romantically involved.

He took his hat in his hand and went to the door. He bowed deeply, and said goodbye, almost in a whisper. Without looking at anyone, he slipped out. A little later he was seen running down the street, without a coat, rather thinly dressed, and with long, uncut hair.

Bodensen remained seated.

IX

It was true, Charlotte and Bondesen saw each other in private, in Bondesen's room in Parkvejen, when no other people were around. She had already been there many times. The first time was when they went home from the Labor Society meeting that evening when Bondesen had so completely captured her heart. Since then she had been there quite often during the autumn and winter. They generally stopped there for an hour or two when they came back from their bicycle excursions, and after the snow had begun to fall they went to the theater or the circus just to be together for a little while afterwards in Bondesen's room. She was so warm after the walk, after the fresh air. She always loosened her clothes when she came in, and Bondesen helped her with this. There was a fire in the stove, and to make it really cozy they would extinguish one of the lamps.

This had been repeated so often that Bondesen's initial intense infatuation began to fade a little. The worst of it was that Charlotte had begun to come up to him on her own, without notice, when she had errands in town. He did not like these public visits. He preferred to take her up himself in a hurry, so as not to meet anyone on the way up to the third floor. When they came to his door, he was obliged to be a little cautious, to stick his nose up the stairs and listen to see if it was quiet on the floors above. This way, it was always a little exciting, a spicy adventure. And when they had happily and comfortably entered his room and closed the door, it was a pleasure for him to breathe out after this little thrilling experience, and to loosen her clothes with feverish hands. All this was gone when she came in the middle of the day with parcels in her hands, smelling of the purchases she had made for her mother in the grocery store. It was just like a woman coming home with meat wrapped in paper for dinner. And how unappealing it was to take off one's clothes in the full light of day from two windows, in the sunshine, when at any moment one might expect the postman or a friend or even the landlady who might have left her duster in there from the morning. No, Bondesen did not like it at all.

Were it not for the fact that he was as good as engaged to Charlotte, he would have declined these visits. She saw nothing, did not understand that his first hot passion was over. She just continued to visit. And she was just as tender and lovely when she left as when she entered. But he could not help it that he no longer rejoiced when she came to the door.

Endre Bondesen sat thinking about all this, and he felt sorry for himself.

Now Fredrik, too, had in a way deceived him, betrayed his trust. He had never dreamed of making him as firm a radical as he himself was. Fredrik had too much willpower for that. But for all the speaking and preaching and pounding the table he had done for his friend, he proved to be an unchanged Ihlen, a right-wing man, a bureaucrat. For this reason, Bondesen would gladly have stayed away from the Ihlens completely, would have made other acquaintances, moved about a little. It became tiresome in the long run to be the constant companion of a single family. But circumstances were against him, and he had to put up with it. Besides, Fredrik was now permanently employed at the *Gazette*, and Bondesen had to hold on to his friendship for that reason. There was no mistaking that he—Bondesen—was carrying around something in his head that he wanted to write, some verses, some poems of more than ordinary significance, and he had all the time imagined making his debut in the *Gazette*, the newspaper that more and more people were reading.

He had thought of going straight home from the Ihlens' house and trying to see if he could not begin on his verses at once. It had been his first thought when he got out of bed that morning. But everything had been spoiled. Perhaps it was foolish to be annoyed, but Bondesen was annoyed all the same. Højbro had agitated him with his long, all-important replies to his remarks, and Charlotte had driven him to reveal their secret relationship to everybody. Now his bonds bound him even tighter, made him unfree, hindered his movements. He was apparently not meant to be in any inseparable relation to anybody, and his engagement, which he had indeed entered into in a moment of weakness and on the spur of the moment, tormented him instead of making him happy.

Mrs. Ihlen came in from the kitchen and began to talk about the spare room. It might happen, she said, that Højbro would leave them one day. She would not want to lose him, for he had been a most excellent tenant, but he had lately become so strange and distant. And when he left, the room would be available.

Bondesen had to think quickly to save himself. He knew that if he moved into the house he would be completely trapped and the full extent of his relationship with Charlotte would be discovered immediately. It would be no different than being married. Nor did he intend to deceive Charlotte. No one would accuse him of having acted so wickedly. They had been in agreement for quite a while, and she had given her word. But lately, he had felt the urge to think it over a little, to reconsider the matter. After all, he might have to take up his studies again and take his exams.

He could not, with his best intentions, answer Mrs. Ihlen other than that he had unfortunately rented in Parkvejen for a longer period, for the whole year, and that he regretted it.

When he heard Fredrik in the next room, he got up to leave. Bondesen was unhappy with everything at that moment. It did not help that Mrs. Ihlen also found it a little suspicious that he had just then rented in Parkvejen for the whole year.

Charlotte looked at him with the same cheerful, trusting eyes. Of all of them, she had suddenly become the happiest, so much had it pleased her that Bondesen had revealed their secret in everyone's presence.

"Thank you," she said, "thank you!"

He put his arm around her. And just a moment before he had wanted to withdraw from her! He did not know where his thoughts had been. He would never do anything to make her unhappy.

Fredrik came into the room looking a little paler than usual, a little strained after the hard work of the last few days with his political articles. This work had taken for more effort than all his scientific papers. He was not a politician and had never taken much interest in politics. When the Left said one thing and the Right another, it could not be otherwise. But it was the Right that was right, he felt faintly in his heart, although he used to say that he also found much justification in the Left's opposition.

But now that Ihlen was on this different track, there was less and less time to devote to his science. The *Gazette* was filled with politics day after day. The Union articles had caused a stir throughout the country. Even the Swedish press had picked them up and made a great deal of money out of them, and every day Lynge was in the field with a defense or an explanation of these articles. And in the midst of all this Ihlen stood almost idle, and could not do much more than make clippings and rewrite short articles. But this work was not in keeping with his interests, and when he went down to the editorial office he wished quite fervently that all of the political squabbling would soon be over.

But that would be a long way off. Lynge had put all other things aside for the time being to defend his new standpoint on Union politics. And he once again showed his skill in the most astonishing way. What had he done? What was the great crime for which all the stupidity of the country now rose up? He had simply stated that the Union was best as it was, and that no man could stand up and take responsibility for the radical change which certain people had proposed. What then? If the Left wanted something other than the Union, it was no longer the Left. It should not come and try to subtly run conservative propaganda under the mask of the Left. The *Gazette* would reject it as unworthy of honest politics. The *Gazette* was the Liberal Party as it had been and as it intended to be, therefore it held on to the Union.

In short, the *Gazette* was so honest and conscientious that Leo Højbro was completely and utterly wrong in his unkind accusations. No one who read the *Gazette* with any understanding could have anything to complain about it.

How beautiful and humane it sounded when the paper protested in the strongest possible terms against the hostile and angry language against the Union! The *Gazette* would no longer be party to this hatred. In the same way that Lynge had considerably improved the tone of his newspaper in other matters, he wanted to refine Norwegian journalism in this respect as well. One went furthest by acting like educated people. And as smoothly as Lynge's pen ran, he was so clearly right in his decisions that the attacks on him gradually subsided. There were few who were not a little affected by this sincere endeavor to raise the level of journalism.

The *Northman* was indeed left behind. Tenaciously and faithfully it held its ground, stuck to its age-old left-wing position, which could show no change, and warned to the best of its ability against this last day's conversion. But the *Northman*'s strength was not in attacking. Its real strength was in explaining its previous statements, something it too often needed to do, when everything it had said and meant was woefully turned upside down right in front of its nose. It was a little awkward, but after these earnest, corrective words the *Northman* said no more. Was it afraid of Lynge? Did it not even dare to give him one of its well-known blows, which caused no man to flinch? So overpoweringly clever was Editor Lynge that few or none dared to move until he had given the signal. Hardly was a scoundrel attacked, an endeavor supported, a book of somewhat dubious content reviewed, a man recommended for a post, before Lynge had given the nod. It was also clearly seen when the *Northman*'s articles on the plight of the sailors were snatched by Lynge. The poor editor of the *Northman* had not said a word, had not asserted his right, and it was never clarified where the articles had actually appeared first. For no one bothered to re-read old newspapers.

But in those days the *Northman* had the unexpected pleasure of seeing its steadfastness rewarded. Dozens of new subscribers poured in, old, faithful leftists who were now leaving the *Gazette*, old veterans, the heart of the party. For the first time Lynge had staged a surprise that the audience did not approve of, and he had never before been so ridiculously wrong in his calculations. But he did not give up, never, and it was to be found that he was the one who had the last laugh after all. He had stuck out his neck a little, and ought one not to be allowed to stick out one's neck a little for a change? Should it not be repaid to him at once? Was not his paper the only paper worth reading? The *Northman*, which was, as it were, on the point of giving it up, flared up again and wanted to live. It got subscribers, and adjusted itself to endure alongside the *Gazette*! Well, let it live. It was, in spite of its imperfections, an old comrade in opinion. Let it live. Lynge should never envy it its poor scraps.

He knew that he had his large audience in the city. Christiania could not do without him. There he was in his element! What did it matter then that a couple of people from Trøndelag or a handful of dead people canceled their subscriptions to his newspaper? Other readers took their place, people whose innermost political opinions he had struck by his changed attitude. Yes, he had weathered worse storms.

He questioned Leporello daily about the town's attitude to the matter: "But what does the town think? What do they say in the Grand?"

The town no longer talked exclusively about the Union articles. Leporello had a suspicion that the *Northman* had once again drawn attention to itself with its reporting of the painter Dalbye's suicide.

This suicide had really gotten people's attention. Dalbye was a young man, well known from Karl Johans gate.* He had already published a collection of poems upon graduating, and to that extent he was considered promising. When he came to Christiania he soon made himself known by a couple of scandals of taste, and a little later he also exhibited a couple of paintings at Blomquist's. Now this young man had gone and shot himself. A member of the *Northman*'s staff had happened to hear the shot and had been the first to announce the sad news, dryly and modestly, without fuss and noise, as was the *Northman*'s habit. The paper had even revealed its sympathy for the unfortunate man whom some secret affliction had driven to his death. No other paper knew of the affair until they saw it in the *Northman*. Where was the *Gazette*, where in the world was it? It had missed a first-page editorial of great importance. And Lynge was more annoyed than he cared to admit that this prey had escaped him.

But what did the town say? Was the city on the painter's side?

As far as Leporello had been able to learn, the city was not particularly upset by the young man's death. His talent was even disputed. Moreover he had half-way compromised a young lady with a well-known name.

Then Lynge seized his pen. The *Northman* was hardly likely to become too arrogant from this story, which it had stumbled upon so

---

*Translator's note: The main street of the city of Christiania (present-day Oslo), Norway, named in honor of Charles III John, who was King of Sweden and Norway from 1818 until his death in 1844.

effortlessly. Again, Lynge attempted to set the public opinion, so that this suicide would almost be regarded as ridiculous, so exaggerated and inflated was it, and he advised the police to ascertain whether other students among the deceased's friends might have prevented this young man from taking his own life. Such things must not be allowed to take place in a society with civilization and morality. One must guard against youths using the revolver on themselves simply because their dinner soup had grown cold.

And at that moment Lynge was once again passionate, inflamed with sympathy for the public spirit and the society that had to endure so much. He put a lot of sound conviction into his lines and found them to be excellent himself. People again came to admire his incomparable ability to quickly and correctly determine his fellow men's innermost opinions on matters. Inflated, that's right! Exaggerated and ridiculous! After all, what did such a youth have to kill himself over?

When Ihlen entered the *Gazette*'s premises he heard loud talking in the editor's office, and the secretary said with a smile:

"He is having a fight with one of his lady friends."

A little later a woman came out of Lynge's office with every sign of agitation. She was heavy and fat, with unusually fair skin and blue eyes. It was Mrs. L., the "Mountain Lady," as she was called, because she was so large and had such white skin.

Lynge followed her bowing to the door. He kept his distance, and even asked her to drop in again one day, knowing full well that after this showdown she would never come back. They could no longer be reconciled. Lynge's volatile temper had caused her too much grief, and he, for his part, looked forward to the day of their parting with anticipation. Now, thank God, it was over! These middle-aged ladies, with whom it always fell to his lot to get involved, had no idea how much embarrassment they inflicted on a man when they would not let go. The woman had even reproached him for certain broken promises, certain unfair remarks, lies. Well, his long life as a journalist had trained him to weather such storms. His inner strength had been so great that he had not even lowered his eyes when she accused him for his breach of faith and promise.

But would he never succeed in conquering a heart that no one else could conquer, the desired, young, radiant girl who would prefer him to anyone else? Would he never succeed? Why couldn't he? He was forty years old, but he felt like a youth. He had even once made Charlotte Ihlen blush before his very eyes.

Then he remembered Fredrik, her brother, whom he had brought into the *Gazette* and he began to wish him away again. He opened his door and looked out, and Ihlen was sitting at his desk. Lynge no longer knew what to do with this man. The newspaper's budget was heavily burdened, and now Ihlen no longer had the interest of the public. People had ceased to marvel at seeing his fine name in Lynge's paper. What then? Of course it was not just for the man's own sake that he had been made a contributor to the *Gazette*, and it was no longer possible to put too much faith in him. There were now the dozens of members of the Left's core troops who had left the *Gazette* and gone over to the *Northman*. Was that a petty matter, a trifle?

Lynge, by the way, could not understand the people who read the *Northman*, that stiff greasy rag that could not draw a line or trap a lawbreaker if its life depended on it. Lynge was the great editor, the great journalist who published the most widely-read paper in the country. He wished his fellow editor all the best, but he stood in his way. Lynge's principle was to make a newspaper read in spite of everything, and the *Northman* defied this principle with its intolerable political stubbornness.

Suddenly Lynge sent for his business manager. A short, thin, black-bearded man entered. He had a small share in the newspaper and was devoted to it with life and soul.

Lynge had heard that the subscribers were beginning to leave them.

Yes, and they were supposed to have gone over to the *Northman*.

Lynge was thinking. This little businessman was also thinking.

"The steamship companies are advertising in the *Northman*," he said.

"Are they?" Lynge replied questioningly.

"Yes, the *Northman* also has advertisements from the canal service at Fredrikshald."

"I see," said Lynge, all at once. "I was not aware of that, to put it plainly. The correct thing to do would be to advertise in the most widespread newspaper, and the most widespread newspaper is the *Gazette*."

It was far from Lynge to want to destroy the life of a fellow member of the Left, but this individual, the *Northman*'s editor, no longer supported him in the old politics of the party. On the contrary, he hampered the *Gazette*'s activities. Therefore he had to fight him. It was a matter of principle.

They talked a little about the lost subscribers, and Lynge was given the number. Many well-known left-wing names were mentioned. Several had expressly given the Union articles as the reason for their termination of the paper.

Before the manager left, a bold plan had ripened behind Lynge's small, contemplative brow.

X

The snow was blowing in drifts in the streets. Castle Hill was filled with smoke. All voices, all sounds, the stamping of hoofs, the ringing of bells, were muffled by the snow, and all lamps glowed with little light. And the people, with their coat collars turned up and their shoulders hunched, made their way through the town, hurrying home, hurrying home.

In the evening, Leo Højbro walked upright and indifferent as a bear through the snow on Castle Hill. He still had no overcoat on and walked without gloves. Occasionally, when his left ear filled with snow, he quickly wiped it off with his red, warm hands and walked slowly on.

Højbro was on his way home from the bank. He had already reached the park road. A door opened quickly, a lady slipped out into the street, and the door closed cautiously behind her. The lady caught sight of him and wanted to retreat, but it was too late. They were at once standing directly opposite each other. He recognized her at once. It was Charlotte, and he greeted her.

Was the lady really out in such weather?

She was anxious and ashamed. Did he have any idea? Højbro was the last person she would want to meet when she came out of Bondesen's door. It was fortunate that the lamps shone so poorly. Otherwise, he would have noticed her embarrassment at once.

She replied with a few words to the effect that she had been running errands in the town, and that it was unfortunately getting late for her. But Højbro spoke so openly and indifferently that she soon became calm herself. He related a little incident from the opening of the Parliament, where he had been present, and this was so amusing that she burst out laughing. She was happy that he had no suspicion of her. No, he suspected nothing when he was so calm.

They braced themselves against the drifting snow and walked on as best they could.

"I don't know whether I dare offer you my arm," he said, "but perhaps you would go a little easier with it."

"Thank you," she said. And she took his arm.

"There's nobody here to see us anyhow," he said.

To this she made no reply. God knows what he meant!

"It is strange how seldom we see you nowadays," she said.

And he answered again, as he had several times before, that work, just work, nightly extra work, kept him busy.

He spoke the truth. During the long evenings while he sat alone in his room, Højbro had half-finished a little work, a sort of philosophical-political pamphlet, in which he had given an account of the Left's ideal striving for full equality in the Union, and at the same time he had attacked Editor Lynge and the *Gazette*'s activities with the fiercest vehemence. Højbro was really working diligently on this little book. Mrs. Ihlen had recently seen him busy until late at night, and he used more and more kerosene for his lamp.

But Charlotte knew nothing of this nocturnal madness. She laughed and said:

"All this work all the time? If only I could believe it!"

He would give her proof at any time, preferably as soon as they got home, if she wanted.

They both laughed and walked on arm in arm. When the wind beat against her skirts she almost stopped, grew heavy, and leaned closer to him. How wonderful it was that she hardly dared to move from the spot! He grew warm and silent with happiness at being able to help her along with his strong arm.

"Are you cold?" he asked.

"No, not now," she replied. "But you are cold?"

"Am I? No, I'm not."

"Your arm is positively trembling."

Well, what if his arm trembled? Was it the cold that made him shiver a little, when he had to push his hat higher and higher on his forehead for the sake of warmth? He suddenly remembered that she was, of course, Bondesen's bride-to-be, another man's fiancée. He answered:

"If my arm trembles, it is not from cold. It has probably grown tired. We can change it."

And he went around to her right side and gave her his other arm.

They struggled on against the snow.

"How you can manage without an overcoat?" she asked.

"As I have managed so far this winter, there will be no need for a coat after this," he said evasively. "In two months it will be spring."

And God knows that Højbro longed for spring. That winter had been the longest in his life, full of suffering and sorrowful days. During the day he stood and worked at his desk at the bank, in perpetual fear that his forged names would be discovered. His boss never said a word to him, never demanded any information without Højbro trembling, certain that soon he would be caught. Sometimes he had the despairing confession on his lips to put an end to it, but when his boss came and he saw this man of honor who had shown him the highest confidence for a number of years, he remained mute, silent as the grave. And one day passed and another came, and there was never an end to his deep torment.

So he struggled through the days.

When he came home in the evenings he became prey to another misery. He lived in the house side by side with the family, and his hopeless passion for Charlotte continued to burn. He heard her footsteps in the parlor, heard her voice when she spoke or hummed, and every time it was as if a flute of fire were playing through his blood. It was painful and delightful, harrowing, full of uneasiness. He listened at the wall, held his breath and listened, tried to guess her actions at every moment, and trembled in happy fear when she passed his door in the hall. Perhaps she would come in now. God knows, she might have an errand. And yet she had never been in his room, never.

No, he would long ago have gone his way, moved far away to the other end of the town, if he had had the means to do so. But until Mrs. Ihlen repaid him the money he had loaned her, the hundred and a half crowns, he could not afford to go anywhere.

With his last penny, and by selling both his watch and coat, he had been able to make his regular payments to the bank. Now he owned nothing, not a shilling. Mrs. Ihlen mentioned one day that Fredrik was now doing very well, and that she would repay the loan as early as the middle of the next month. So the rest of his debts were soon to be settled, and the dangerous paper with the false names written on it would be buried and forgotten forever at last. And soon the spring would come with its bright days and bright, silent nights. My God, how welcome it would be!

"We are almost home," said Charlotte suddenly.

"Yes, we are."

She looked up at him, but could not see his face. He had said this "yes" so strangely, almost sadly, almost tonelessly. She laughed and said:

"You didn't mind walking in the cold tonight?"

"No, because you were with me," he answered without hesitation. Then he regretted his answer, took two or three too hasty steps forward, and said, abruptly, "Nonsense! How I slur my words! Well, now we are home."

He opened the door and let her go ahead up the stairs. Mrs. Ihlen met them in the hall.

"God, Charlotte, where have you been for so long?" she asked reproachfully.

Højbro stepped in at once. He laughed and said:

"You must forgive us. We have been walking. Miss Charlotte and I have been walking."

And Mrs. Ihlen clapped her hands together. What magnificent walking weather they had chosen!

Højbro said nothing more, Charlotte looked at him sideways. Did he know where she had been after all, and did he want to cover for her? She could have dropped to the ground.

But Mrs. Ihlen put an end to the embarrassment by opening the parlor door and ushering the snowy people in. Højbro had no outer garments to remove. He was hustled in covered in snow. Yes, yes, right in. They had a visitor, so now he really had to be friendly for a change!

A young, remarkably beautiful lady was sitting on the sofa. She had stopped at the Ihlens on her way home from town. She lived farther out on Hægdehaugen, and it was Charlotte she had come to visit. Her forehead was exceedingly white and her eyes green and shining. Around her neck she wore a black velvet ribbon, just like a child. Højbro immediately settled down and entertained the ladies in his best manner. Little by little he became lively, had much to talk about, and altogether showed himself from a new side. Both Charlotte and Sofie were surprised by this change in him. He knew himself why he was acting so cheerfully. The strange lady must not lack entertainment. On the contrary, she must be shown a really interesting time. He had always shown Charlotte a great deal of attention. However, tonight no one would suspect him. He knew how to control himself.

Charlotte looked at him repeatedly. The cold outside had put a strong color in his face. He was radiant, and his words sparkled. Finally, she reminded him that he had promised her some proof of his nighttime writing. Might she be allowed to see it?

Yes, he would fetch it at once. And he rose to his feet.

No, couldn't she come with him? Charlotte got up too. Then it would be less trouble for him?

"No!" he said curtly.

She sat back down quietly.

Højbro was already out the door. What was going on with her? Tonight she wanted to come into his room, to talk to him? What did that mean? Yes, he knew that tonight he had impressed her. His heart was full now.

He came back with his pamphlet, spread out the handwritten pages, and said:

"Well, here is the proof of my little night work. Haha, it doesn't look like much to you, does it? No, I'm not used to writing. I give it a lot of thought, and that's why it goes so slowly. But I really have been working on this in the evenings."

Sofie asked, "What is it?"

"What would I call it?" he replied. "A political writing, truly, a little warning, a blast on the horn, from the point of view of the common man."

"Well, I think it would be amusing to read sometime, at any rate."

"No, no," he said. "God knows whether it will come to anything at all. But I will finish it sooner or later."

"I am sure it will be good," said Charlotte softly. How could she know? He blushed, he was even moved, said thank you with an awkward smile, and turned again to the young lady on the sofa. He continued where he had left off when he was interrupted, telling her the hunting adventure he had begun. The lady noticed the odor of pine throughout the room. She, too, was from the country, and had only been in Christiania for the last year. She could clearly understand his delight in the forest and the field, and in all things under the open sky. She spoke in a soft, singing voice.

There were footsteps in the hall. Fredrik had come home.

Fredrik was not in the best of moods. Since the Parliament had opened, matters had deteriorated still further for him. There was no longer any prospect of getting the slightest bit of his science articles published. The *Gazette* was again a purely political organ, with editorials on all important matters and the fiercest attacks on the government every day.

The administration which had begun so well, which once had the hero and idol of the people as its head, faltered more and more. It would hardly endure the current parliamentary period, and no one was more eagerly interested in its downfall than the *Gazette*. These were indeed troubled times: a ministry that was hated and cursed by all the liberal papers for its treacherous conduct, that was sinking under the weight of everyone's contempt, that stood or fell by the grace of the people which hesitated to give it the death blow, not to mention a divided Left that quarreled among themselves about the implementation of the latest major reform measures, the transition of old politicians from one party to the other, and turmoil and confusion and failing opinions on all sides. Ihlen had never in his life lived in such turbulent times. It became more and more apparent to him that party politics was not his forte, and he struggled more and more not to give up writing completely.

Little by little he had drifted from writing about juniper oil for medical use—something in which there was frankly no general interest—to articles on the House Council for Diseases, and extracts from popular medical books. He sank deeper and deeper, writing about the state of cleanliness in the streets, about sewerage, and ended up with an article on the treatment of livestock in the market squares. It was impossible to go any lower. What a distance from his National Question of two million to this warning to the butchers of Cristiania to keep their slaughtered animals clean. But to crown his humiliation, Lynge had now demanded that he should report from the Parliament, and thus he unfortunately had to deprive him of his regular salary and put him on a per-column payment for all small original articles. All this had just happened as he was leaving the office.

Ihlen was downcast. His mother asked:

"But would it be so bad to be paid by the column?"

"No, Mother," he replied. "It could be very good if they would only print what I wrote."

There was silence in the room. Even Højbro sat silent for a moment. Mrs. Ihlen would no longer be able to pay him back the little loan, and what would happen to his installments at the bank next month? He would not show any sadness tonight, come what might! Then he went over to Fredrik, talked cheerfully with him, and said that once one had got into the habit of writing for his column, he might find it much better. He would be more his own master, and he could also work at home. "Yes," said Fredrik, " I will try it."

The young lady on the sofa got up to leave. Højbro offered to accompany her home, and the lady thanked him heartily for his kindness. But surely it would be a pity to drag him out into the storm again.

Not a bit! Oh, it would a pleasure to him to be a trifle sprinkled with snow!

But then Charlotte got up, too, and dragged her mother into a corner. She would like to go too. Couldn't she? Just this once?

What a notion! What was the matter with Charlotte this evening? She wanted to go out again. She begged with blank eyes to be allowed to follow these people out into the snow. The mother shook her head, and Charlotte continued to plead in a whisper.

Højbro also understood what she had in mind. He shook his head and said with a smile:

"Oh no, it really isn't the weather for you tonight, Miss." She gave him a quick, sad look, and sat back down in her chair.

When Højbro came home that evening after having accompanied the strange lady home, he heard that Charlotte was still awake and sitting up in her room.

XI

In the morning Charlotte followed her brother down to the editorial office. He was to be at a meeting at half-past nine, and he was rather despondent. What was the use of all he had learned and written when he was now employed in creating slanderous anecdotes about the Parliament?

The editor had not yet arrived. The secretary handed Charlotte some illustrated magazines and journals from the *Daily Post* to leaf through for the time being. A little later the editor appeared at the door.

He whistled, his hat was a little askew, and altogether he seemed to be in good spirits. He greeted them with a smile, said a few joking, friendly words to Ihlen, and begged him not to forget his pencil when he went to the meeting.

"It is not intended that you should remain at this tedious work," he said, "but I beg you to do me this favor today. For I have had to send a man up to Jævnaker on the occasion of Bjørnson's meeting."

Then he went into his office.

A little later he opened the door again and said:

"Won't you come in here and sit down, Miss Ihlen?"

Charlotte went. She was really very fond of Lynge, who had always shown her the greatest kindness. After her brother had peeped in at the door and said that he was going to the meeting, she sat quietly in her seat and talked to the editor, who now and then read a letter or glanced through a telegram.

Suddenly he stopped. He got up and walked around to her side, where he stood looking at her. She was leafing through an illustrated newspaper. She glanced up at him and blushed bright red. He stood there with his head tilted slightly to one side and his hands behind his back. His eyes were half closed as he looked down at her.

"What splendid hair you have!" he said softly, and laughed tremblingly.

She could no longer remain seated. Her head was buzzing, and the room began to sway. She stood up, and at that very moment she felt his arms around her, and he breathed into her face.

She gave a little strangled cry. She heard him say, "No, hush!" and with that she sank down on the chair again. She had a faint feeling that he must have kissed her.

He once more leaned down to her. She heard him speak again. He addressed her in hushed, intimate words, and when he tried to put his arms around her, to touch her, under the pretense of helping her up, she gathered all her strength and pushed him back. Then she got up. She said not a word, and shuddered violently.

"There, there!" he said soothingly, and laughed again with a suppressed, trembling giggle.

She opened the door at once and left. She was dazed and knew so little what she was doing that she even waved goodbye to him.

When she reached the door she began cry. She was still trembling, and she didn't regain her composure until she had reached the top of Castle Hill.

Now it was best to put an end to it. It was as if everybody knew what she was and could address her in the worst ways. She would tell Bondesen everything and ask him to announce their engagement at once, and then they could marry later when they chose.

For a moment she thought of Højbro. Yes, of course he knew all about her. Hadn't he just stepped forward and covered for her yesterday? It had come to that. Later in the evening, by the way, Højbro had been positively rude to her, answered her coldly and dismissively. He could not have answered a maid more contemptuously, and yet he had been very good to her before. Then he had gone home with Mimi, had followed this strange person home in the snow and storm. Well, why shouldn't he have done it? She—Charlotte—for her part was not surprised. But Mimi had short hair, and Højbro had once expressly said that he did not like ladies with short hair. Why then did he go home with Mimi?

Then she remembered what had happened earlier, in the previous hour. It had already become like a dream to her, and she stopped in the middle of the castle park and wondered if the incident down at the editorial office had really happened. What had Lynge been talking about? About a meeting in the evening? Did he not make a few tickling strokes across her breast when he tried to raise her up? What if it was all her imagination? She was no longer sure of her situation. She was exhausted after a long night of despair. She really had not slept an hour. Perhaps, after all, Lynge had said nothing to her. Perhaps he had only wanted to reassure her when she imagined she felt his arms around her. God forbid that it was all a lie! At any rate, she no longer remembered how she had gotten out of the office and down into the street.

She did not find Bondesen at home.

With a heavy heart she went on her way. She would see Bondesen in the evening. She could not wait any longer now. Their affairs had to be settled at once. Her thoughts were still occupied with Lynge. Perhaps he had not said anything to her, and she had only deceived herself. But he had kissed her. She still felt it. By God, he had done it! And as she walked homeward she spat several times in the street.

As she stepped into the hall she saw, to her astonishment, Bondesen, who had just then rushed out of Højbro's room. They looked at each other for a moment. He lost his composure briefly, and then said quickly:

"You were not at home. I have been looking for you all over the house. I even looked in Højbro's room."

"Did you want to see me?" she asked.

"Not exactly. I only wanted to say good morning. I didn't see you yesterday."

She heard her mother coming. She quickly got Bondesen out into the hall and pulled the front door shut behind them.

They walked down the street together, hardly speaking. Each had his own things to think about.

When they reached Bondesen's room, Charlotte sat down on the sofa, and Bondesen beside her on a chair. For the first time in this place she kept her coat on. Then she began to talk about what was on her mind. It was necessary that there be a change in this. People saw it all and despised her.

Saw it? Who saw it?

Everybody, Højbro, Lynge, God knows whether Mimi Arentzen had not also noticed something. She had looked at her suspiciously the previous night.

Bondesen laughed and said that it was nonsense.

Nonsense? No, unfortunately, and he was to believe her. She suddenly said in a choked voice that even Lynge had been very touchy with her today.

Bondesen was startled. Lynge? Did she say Lynge?

Yes, Lynge.

What had he done?

My God, why was he tormenting her? Lynge had touched her, kissed her.

"Lynge?" Bondesen's mouth gaped in astonishment. "Damn it all to hell, Lynge himself!" he said.

Charlotte looked at him.

"It doesn't seem to trouble you much," she said.

Bondesen was silent.

"I just want to tell you," he replied, "that Lynge is not the same as just anybody else."

She opened her eyes wide.

"What do you mean by that?" she said at last.

He shook his head hastily and impatiently, and answered:

"Nothing, nothing! Why are you so bothered by this, Charlotte?"

"What on earth do you mean?" she cried, and threw herself down on the sofa, shaking with horror.

Bondesen had been utterly unable to prevent his feelings for Charlotte from dwindling more and more day by day. During the last month he had even considered whether, after what had passed between them, he should enter into a relationship which was inwardly against him, or whether he should openly and honestly break off their engagement. Was it so unheard of to break off such a little engagement? Were there not open and honest break-ups in all relations in life? How was it with the *Gazette*? When it could no longer serve the Union policy of hatred and fraternal dislike, it stepped forward manfully and broke away. What else could he himself—Bondesen—do as an honest man towards Charlotte? Was it fair to himself and to her that they should enter into a lifelong relationship based on lies and secret indifference?

He had really considered everything conscientiously, and for some time his doubts had been strong. Now he had come to the conclusion that the best thing for both of them was to part amicably.

He even felt that his worth as a human being was increased by this decision. He felt the power of truth within him, became strong and high in the consciousness that he was acting appropriately.

While Charlotte was still sobbing, he said as gently as possible:

"Please stand up and listen to me calmly. I would like to tell you something."

"I suppose you don't love me anymore, Endre," she said very softly.

To this he made no reply. He patted her hair and said:

"Let me explain myself a little..."

She looked up at him. Her eyes were dry, but she was still shaking.

"Is it really true? Tell me, don't you love me? Answer me, answer me!"

He got the inner strength to tell her gently and truthfully that he did not love her as much as before, not fully as much. No, he did not, unfortunately. He could not help it. She must believe him. But he still valued her highly.

There was silence for a few minutes. Charlotte uttered a few whimpers. Her head fell forward on her breast, and she did not move a muscle.

It really pained him to see her so sad for his sake. He took it into his head to belittle himself for her, so that in the end she could be happy. He was not worthy of her. She had lost nothing, nothing. But he thought, as an honest man, that he must tell her the truth while there was still time. Then she could do as she liked with him.

Again there was a long silence. Charlotte put her hands to her forehead. The pause lasted so desperately long that he seized his hat from the table and began to stroke it.

Then with a jerk she took her hands from her face, looked at him with a stiff, sinister smile, and asked:

"Would you like me to go now?"

He jumped up and put his hat back on the table. Good God, could one not take the matter with a little less solemnity? After all, weren't there breaches in all the relations of life?

"No, there is no hurry," he answered, a bit sharply, so as not to lose any of his determination.

She got up and went to the door. He called her back. They must part as friends, he said. She must forgive him. But she opened the door at once, and stepped out without saying a word, without glancing back at him. He heard her footsteps on the creaking steps, further and further down, on the second floor, on the first floor, and at last he stood behind the curtain by the window and saw her come out onto the street. Her hat was still crooked, for she had thrown herself headlong down on the sofa. Then she disappeared around the corner. How crooked her hat was!

Bondesen breathed a sigh of relief. Now it was over. What troubles he had had during the last month, and what a host of stratagems he had struggled with in order to get this unhappy relationship sorted out in the best possible way. Now the conflict was at an end.

For half an hour Bondesen sat motionless in his chair and thought about what had happened. He was genuinely sorry to have had to give Charlotte this heavy blow, as it were, right in the face. It would have suited him better, it would have been more to his liking only to hint at the break-up, to proceed with delicacy. But she herself had asked, and he had had to answer.

There was no doubt that as a human being one relied on being true to oneself. He could not blame himself except that he had fallen in love with this young girl rashly at one time. There was the mistake. That was how it all began. But could anyone deny the heart its right to indulge in rash impulses?

Bondesen finally remembered that he had not yet had lunch. As he walked down through the castle park he was still thinking over the sad scene up in his room. He remembered everything so clearly, everything she had said and what he had answered. He also remembered that he met Charlotte in her entrance hall. She had almost surprised him in Højbro's room.

What a shady fellow this Højbro was! His whole table was full of drafts and written pages. He wanted to be published by none other than Lynge. God help him! He would be crushed, ground between Lynge's fingers.

So Lynge had kissed her. Lynge! Who ever heard of such a brave devil? Who would think it?

Lynge had been sitting for several hours doing very little, but when he came down to the editorial office with his copy, it turned out that he had managed to get at least two columns of gossip and slander ready. He had never made money so easily before. Lynge read through the article immediately and found it excellent.

Charlotte had fallen into a deep sleep when she came home. She had been asleep for several hours. Now she was pale, and shivered a little with cold, but otherwise she felt perfectly well.

Ihlen asked her if she had been ill down at the *Gazette* earlier that day. What was it that had happened to her?

She answered her brother that she had felt unwell, yes. But it had passed when she came out into the street.

"Lynge was quite worried about you," said Fredrik.

"Really?"

Pause.

And then she suddenly surprised her brother by declaring that she would never again follow him down to the editorial office. When he pressed her for an explanation, she said that she would be embarrassed to see Lynge again. It was awkward to be embarrassed, so to speak, in the presence of strangers.

XII

Lynge was annoyed with himself that he had let his feelings towards Charlotte run away with him. Not that he believed that he had gone a hair's breadth further than he could defend if he had to, but it was still unpleasant to be rejected, belittled, and to have to withdraw with unfinished business. He was always spurned, always rejected. Only with the more affected, the ordinary women, did he gain a somewhat narrow entrance. If he came to them in his turn, he was let in.

It annoyed him all the more for Charlotte's sake, as he could not free himself from a little anxiety. He had never before dared to try his luck with young ladies of her class. No one know what she might do. She had relatives, a large family, and one could be swindled for it, knocked off one's perch. Well, at any rate, there was no third party present, and so there was no proof.

But he was resentful of the whole affair. For some time, he had overlooked her brother's incompetence. Fredrik Ihlen's articles about the Parliament were in reality so impossible that he would be a laughing stock if he printed them. But he would have to print them, and even pay an exorbitant price for them, in order to get peace in his heart.

Lynge swore that never again should a young lady entice him into a sexual affair.

Of course, he would never abandon his admiration for women in general, even if it was only for the more common ones. Mrs. Dagny had stopped him in the street that morning, and with just a handshake and one of her sweet smiles had rekindled his old fondness for her. She had been more than gracious, and said that she had regretted that she saw him so seldom lately, that she missed him, and that she even had something to talk to him about, something she had been thinking about lately.

They agreed to go to the theater together in the evening, and afterwards he was to go home with her. Lynge waited with longing for the evening. However, a slight uneasiness had come over him. He threw away the newspaper he was reading and frowned. The miserable, scheming washerwoman from Hammersborg had not yet ceased to trouble him. She had finally had her appeal printed in another paper, and she had not concealed the fact that this cry of distress had been refused publication in the *Gazette*.

Lynge shrugged his shoulders. Now he must surely be rid of this beggar woman, who had the audacity to present herself to him with less than a clean face! But there you are, was there any gratitude in the world? Had the woman also expressly pointed out that he—Editor Lynge—had extended her a considerable sum of at the very beginning? Absolutely not. The woman had not done so. Refused publication in the *Gazette!* That was all.

As soon as Lynge had finished what was necessary for the morning edition, he left the office. He had to go to the barber's, and afterwards straight to Mrs. Dagny's. But first he had an errand to attend to. Lynge took the road down to the *Northman*'s offices.

He had, unfortunately, another little unpleasant affair to put in order, but this matter did not affect him in any embarrassing way. The fact was that his business manager, out of sheer concern for the *Gazette*'s well-being, had gone and made a stupid blunder. The manager had sent out a notice to the subscribers, comparing the number of subscribers of the *Gazette* and the *Northman*, and urging the public to advertise in the most widely circulated paper. He had conceived this plan on his own, but had carried it out so crudely and openly, without so much as hinting at a question of principle, that the editor himself had to intervene. Imagine if the *Northman* took offense this time and made a fuss? What if it exposed the sloppiness against a fellow opinion-maker, against an honestly competing publication? Lynge would not for all the world want that kind of crudeness to be associated with his newspaper.

He quickly finished with the *Northman*'s editor. He came roaring into the unknown editorial office like the most distinguished cock in town, said so and so, it was an indignity, a shame, he knew nothing about it until now, apologized and promised to prevent any further recurrence. Thus everything was settled. The *Northman*'s editor said the few words that needed to be said, nodded the few nods that needed to be nodded, and let the matter drop. In his heart he was even glad that he was so lucky to be able to do his great colleague a favor.

Lynge said goodbye and left. But the *Northman*'s editor immediately went to his secretary and reported what had happened. He felt the need to confide in someone, and there was no one else but the secretary at hand.

Lynge had done the deed. He walked at an easy gait, with his hat on, down the street, and stopped at his barber's. A little while later he came out again, shaved, brushed, greatly rejuvenated and happy. But now he had the afternoon off. He had no work to do, nothing to look after. After he had gone a little way down the street he realized that he had no gloves on. He had left them behind him at the barber's. Oh, yes, of course! Why the devil, he had forgotten his cuffs, too!

Annoyed, he turned back, and a few minutes later he saw his wife. She was coming straight towards him. As there was no way of moving aside, he couldn't avoid her. She stared him straight in the face as she came walking along.

He greeted her with a nod and said:

"Well, are you in town?"

"Yes," she replied. "Listen, won't you come with me to the theater tonight? I have such a fancy to see a show."

He jumped.

The theater? No, he could not.

Oh well! She had really had such a desire.

She could go alone, couldn't she?

She hesitated, but thoughtfully agreed. But why couldn't he go too, just for once? It was not often that she asked him.

No, he had a meeting tonight.

Yes, but only for a couple of acts? Surely he could at least accompany her there?

He shook his head, and said, a little impatiently, that it would be best to leave his pleasures behind when he had other matters to attend to. There was no time for any frivolities.

She stood for a moment.

"Well, well, I'll have to go alone then," she said.

"Yes, you do that. Listen, couldn't you take one of the children with you? Oh no, it's true, it's not for children tonight. Yes, yes. I have left my gloves at the barber's. I must go up and fetch them."

They parted.

It was a stroke of luck after all that he had met his wife before he went to the theater. Of course, she had bumped into him before, both at the theater and at a concert, without saying anything, even though he had had some other lady with him. At any rate it was a damper on him, a restraint, and he did not feel like taking any chances that evening.

When Lynge entered Mrs. Dagny's sitting room, she greeted him with a faintly cheerful exclamation. It was good of him to have taken the time to check on her again, in such troubled times.

There was another person present, a Miss Gude, a lady with very white hair. Lynge greeted her cordially. He had met her once before there. She lived with Mrs. Dagny as a sister, as a companion. Miss Gude, however, immediately left the room. She always did so when visitors came.

The lamps were lighted, a red bulb hung glowing by the corner of the sofa, and on the other side of the wall, on a table, stood a lamp with a white light and a white silk shade. It burned cheerfully.

Mrs. Dagny sat down on the sofa under the red lamp, and Lynge seated himself on a chair opposite her. They talked about the latest news of the town, an assault out in Sandviken, about which the *Gazette* had seen fit to publish a large editorial that morning. How cruel people could be to each other! Mrs. Dagny shuddered when she thought about it. She lived there on the entire floor, all alone with Miss Gude and the maid. How possible it would be that an accident would come to her too!

Lynge laughed and said:

"All alone, three grown-up people!" But he assured her that if such a misfortune should happen, surely no one would have the heart to do her any harm once they saw her. He could not believe that. She would rather not be in his shoes! Anonymous letters, threats and insults, almost every day!

And Mrs. Dagny trembled again.

Think of it! What did he do with such letters?

Lynge shrugged his shoulders and replied indifferently:

"I hardly ever read them."

"Think of it! That you should be so bold to take such a stand!"

And he answered haughtily:

"Yes! One is in danger wherever one goes."

Then Mrs. Dagny suddenly remembered that they were going to the theater, and jumped up. She had almost forgotten!

Lynge looked at the clock. He hesitated a little in his answer. It was in fact rather late, and the first act would at any rate be over. He gave the same excuse to Mrs. Dagny as he did to his wife. He had to go to a night meeting before he went home, one he could not fail to attend. But Mrs. Dagny must not be angry with him. He would so earnestly like to go another time, she understood that, preferably the following night. She had to forgive him that he had unfortunately had to stay in the office for so long. There was so much to do at present.

Mrs. Dagny sat down again, resigned. "Another evening then. And no more excuses!"

But Lynge's nocturnal meeting made her curious. She wanted to know something more about it. Would he really leave her and go to a meeting? How important and mysterious this man was! What areas did he not cover in his business! She said:

"So you really only came to say that you can't go to the theater tonight?"

"No," he replied, "not really. I came here first of all because you have been so kind as to give me permission to do so, and secondly to hear what it was you wanted to talk to me about."

"Yes," she said, "if I only dared to say it so straightforwardly." Then she told Lynge what had been on her mind. Well, you see, her husband was gone now. He was away on a trip, and would be home in a few months. She had wanted to make him a little happy when he came home. Perhaps she had not been quite as good as she ought to have been while he had been away. Well, that could be left unsaid for the present. But now she had thought that Lynge, with his enormous influence at the Ministry, could help her a little with this...

Lynge shook his head. Did she want her husband promoted?

No, that wouldn't do, would it? Would it? She didn't understand that at all. But she would have liked to do something for her husband. She frankly said—it was shameful to ask it—but she had thought of an order for him, a cross?

Lynge burst into laughter and said:

"An order? Your husband an order? Do you put a price on such things?"

She shook her head vehemently. "No, no, no!" she cried. "Not me, you know that. But my God, he would appreciate it. He is one of them, after all."

"Yes," said Lynge.

Both were silent for a moment.

"It's just unfortunate," he continued, "that the present ministry will soon be gone, and a right-wing ministry will take its place, and I will be capable of next to nothing in the hands of such a ministry."

"How sad!" she said at last. "Otherwise you might have done it, mightn't you? Tell me, would you have wanted to do it otherwise?"

"I would certainly want to do all I could," he replied.

"Thank you!"

This gratitude went to his heart. He asked:

"Does it grieve you very much that you cannot please your husband with such a surprise now?"

"Yes, indeed, very much," she replied, almost in tears. "I should have liked to see him happy. For, to tell you the truth, I have been happy many, many times while he has been away . . ."

"Well, then, we won't talk about it anymore!"

She changed to a more cheerful tone. "May I ask you about another thing?"

"Of course you may!"

"What is this meeting you are going to tonight? Will you tell me?"

"It is a political meeting," he answered without hesitation.

"A political meeting? So late at night? Is something special going on? "

And again he replied without hesitation:

"It concerns the fall of the Ministry. We need to discuss the day and the circumstances."

Lynge did not want to admit that his political dominance had suffered a slight setback. Within the leading Left Party, some had begun to suspect the great editor. Ever since his famous Union articles, they did not really know where he stood. Conferences were held without him, the President of the Parliament had not visited him once since the opening of the Parliament, and Lynge was no longer indispensable. Now he had an inkling that secret meetings were being held here and there among the leaders, and he was in the same spirit. He participated as before, said his apt words, and, as usual, did not waver an inch in his principles. There was certainly a conference this evening. Leporello had sniffed it out, and the Ministry's fall was certainly to be discussed. At such an event he must be present, of course.

"Just think, the fall of the Ministry!" said Mrs. Dagny.

She fell into thought. She remembered so clearly how highly this ministry had been praised some years ago, the first liberal ministry in the country's history. Her father, Provost Kielland, knew the head of the Ministry personally. How often had he spoken to his children about this mighty Norwegian warrior whose equal had not yet been born in this country! The country had for a long time resounded with his voice. The people's hearts had trembled with enthusiasm when he uttered his words of battle. And now he was to fall! God in heaven, how sad it all was when not even such a man could stand! Imagine simply throwing him away now that he has worn out all his strength in working for the Fatherland!

Mrs. Dagny felt deeply sorry for him. She said:

"But must the Ministry finally fall then? The leader too?"

Lynge answered briefly, without a trace of sentimentality:

"Naturally."

There was a long silence.

Then he would fall! Then he would be forgotten, never mentioned again, never greeted in the street. He would be like a dead man. Mrs. Dagny trembled at the very thought. She had become so heartily afraid of all catastrophes. Since the terrible incident with the adventurer Nagel last year she had not been able to endure shocks of any kind. And here fell Norway's fiercest genius, and was thrown away as if useless. Every scrap of newspaper in the country would announce the tragedy and then be silent about him forever.

"God, how pitiful it all is!" she said at last.

The genuine sadness in her words made him take notice. His sympathetic heart trembled. He looked at her with misty eyes and said:

"Yes, I think so too, but . . ."

She rose suddenly from the sofa, came forward straight to his chair, folded her hands over his shoulders, and said:

"Can't you save him? You can do it!"

He was bewildered. Her nearness, her words, the odor of her breath confused him for a moment.

"Me?" he said.

"Yes, yes . . . oh, if you could!"

"I don't think I can," he said. When he reached for her hands, she withdrew slowly, began to pace back and forth with her head down, and left him sitting alone again. "He could have obeyed the will of the people and been more honest," Lynge said. "Then he would have been able to live out his life."

"Yes, I suppose so." Mrs. Dagny sat down again on the sofa. Then she said: "But will it be so much better to have a pure right-wing government?"

"One which has not broken faith and laws, yes," he replied.

But Lynge nevertheless came to think of his words. Was it so much better from the Left's point of view to have a pure right-wing government? After a long silence he said:

"But you are right about that, by the way. It struck me what you said."

She lay back on the sofa. Her eyes rested on him like two blue stars. Lynge was angry. Women were difficult for him to understand. This man who was so strict and unyielding, whose firmness of principle had long been known, who so ruthlessly purged society of all mischief, this man wavered in his soul at the sound of a woman's voice. She was right. It was perhaps not so much better to have a pure right-wing government. And now his quick head immediately began to work. All the possibilities in the world flashed through his brain. He gathered the broken parties, arranged ingenious and laboriously constructed combinations like houses of cards, appointed ministers, directed, commanded, ruled the country...

He stood up, unable to remain calm any longer, and said in an uneasy voice, trembling with emotion:

"You have put me on to something, ma'am. I admire you beyond measure. I am going to do something."

She got up too. She did not question him about anything. He would probably not have said anything more, so opaque as this man was, but now she held out her hand to him and let him hold it. And she exclaimed, moved by his passion, his cunning:

"God, what a great man you are!"

A quarter of an hour, even five minutes earlier, these words would have excited him to approach this young woman again, but now he had once more become the editor, the public personage, absorbed only by his plans, obsessed by the desperate coup he was contemplating. His eyes were distant. These boyish eyes rested fixed and somber on the lamp with the white silk shade, and a little twitching passed over his forehead. She wanted once more to mention the order, the cross, to say that it was a childish whim of hers, and beg him to forget it, but she did not want to bother him, and besides, he had probably already forgotten it. It was only when she was standing in the doorway, and Lynge was already outside, that she could not restrain herself. She said:

"And this business about the cross was too foolish. We'll forget it, do you hear? We'll forget it."

Then his old desire returned, his love grew stronger, and he quickly took the woman by the waist. And when she stepped back, guarding herself, he responded:

"Are we forgetting? I am not in the habit of forgetting."

Then he said goodnight and left. She stood on the staircase and called down to him:

"Then we shall see each other again, won't we?"

And he answered in a low voice:

"In a few days."

Lynge walked pensively down towards the *Gazette* office.

His head was still buzzing, plans were being made, great decisions were being reached. Time after time he was on the point of bumping into people in the street. It was only eleven o'clock. The town was still awake and all the lights were burning.

Yes, Lynge was going to surprise the country. In spite of everything, contrary to what he had worked for month after month, he would save the Ministry. He would speak out for a radical reconstruction, he would keep the chief and one or two of the councilors of state. The rest would be replaced with new men, all in order to prevent a right-wing government. Could a true Leftist act differently? Could he defend inflicting a right-wing government on the country now that major reforms were about to be implemented? Lynge had already decided on the outstanding Leftists who were to enter the new council. His list of ministers was complete, and he would himself give the individuals instructions when the time came.

And once again the *Northman* and the dogmatic Liberal leaders would gnash their teeth with resentment at having their decisions reversed. Oh, how they would grumble! What then? Was he not accustomed to ride out storms? He had to show the good people that they could not exclude him, Editor Lynge, from their nightly meetings without consequence. They wanted to ignore him, to keep him back. He was anxious to see who would win by this sort of self-righteousness. Had he not for nearly half his life served the country and the party as a slave?

Lynge did not deny that at this moment there had been a change in the people's confidence in his politics. They had certainly changed. He could see that. He no longer had them all in his pocket. They were divided. They were both for and against him. He was controversial. And it all came from the unfortunate articles about the Union. Well, he wanted to teach the people to think things over. He had again put an iron in the fire, and he was going to let the hammer swing on it, play on it, so that the whole world would be astonished. Out in the country, the name of the Prime Minister was still dear. People who had heard his praise all their lives could not tear him out of their hearts. Now Lynge would come like a storm, fire off rockets, swing his hat again, and raise the old great man to his pinnacle once again to the accompaniment of loud music. The people would listen to these sounds. They were familiar tones. There was power in them, and the people would cheer along as before, as in the old days. Yes, Lynge knew what he was doing.

We shall see you again, won't we? Yes, they would see each other again. For these few days he was to do Mrs. Dagny a favor that no one else in the country had the power to do for her. She was to be silenced, to bow to his will. He would also do himself a small favor. He would bring himself into the minds of the people so that he would not easily be forgotten again. The attention he was about to arouse would indemnify him for a long time, and he was already thinking of a small expansion of the *Gazette*, a one-page supplement, which the thousands of new subscribers who were sure to be added would welcome at the beginning of the next quarter.

What would people say? The newspapers, his colleagues, his competitors, the left-wing press would be outraged. Why not? It was precisely a quarrel about his name and his paper that he wanted. Besides, he knew the Left press. It had always agreed with what he had published, and it had the most honorable group of editors whose strengths were not precisely in their heads. He had so often dazzled them. They nodded and did as he said. The only one who would perhaps balk and ask for time to think matters over was the *Northman*. When Lynge announced his reconstruction of the Ministry, the *Northman*'s editor would for a moment be stunned, and then he would say the words that needed to be said, whisper his misgivings with the utmost consideration, and stand firm on his position. Yes, Lynge knew him, and if the *Northman* dared to accuse him of vacillating, he would get his answer. No, he was not waffling. It was precisely in his duty as a firm leftist that he took this step. It was simply politics. The same march, but a different beat.

Lynge had come right up to his office door when he stopped and thought it over. It was really no use doing anything that evening as the *Gazette*'s morning edition was already full, and he might perhaps need the night to consider the details of it. He was on the point of turning back when, out of habit, he opened the letterbox and took in the mail that had arrived.

He went inside and looked through the letters by the light of a lantern. He noticed a large yellow envelope with a salmon-colored seal and opened it curiously.

Lynge jerked abruptly. He even held his breath for a moment. The Prime Minister! The head of the Ministry wanted a talk with him as soon as possible, night or day. The letter had been sent by messenger.

How fortunate that he had come to the editorial office by pure instinct! A conversation night or day! Something was going on. Perhaps his Excellency was wavering. Well, how much better, how much greater then would be Lynge's victory! Although he had missed the secret deliberations of the party leaders, he nevertheless got his nightly meeting. The Prime Minister himself had summoned him.

Lynge took a cab and drove straight down to Toldbodgaden.

There he got out and walked on foot to Stiftsgaarden. He looked around. The street was deserted, and no one saw him. He rang the bell and the gate opened. He was expected and was admitted without waiting.

The old, white-haired Prime Minister received him in a private room.

"I have taken the liberty of inconveniencing you because something important is going on," he said. "I thank you for coming."

This voice, this voice! Lynge had heard it before, in the courtroom, on the podium, in front of large crowds of people. Lynge trembled.

They sat down opposite each other.

"I thought," said the Prime Minister, "that you would perhaps go down to your editorial office this evening when you came from the discussions."

Lynge responded with a bow. At such an event as this meeting, he had, of course, been present.

"I am sorry to say," the Minister continued, "that there has been much disagreement between you, Mr. Editor, and me lately. I apologize for this, and I am by no means free from error. In the difficult transition when the country's first left-wing government took over the reins of power, we councils of state also had more work than anyone could have imagined to avoid failing and the ground was slippery, Mr. Editor. I do not say this as an excuse, but I think there is something to be said for it."

"Of course, Your Excellency."

But no irreparable mistake had been made, persisted the Minister in the same confidential tone. With a little goodwill, everyone would see it and history would judge. Many things could be corrected immediately. His years of hard work had shown his untiring will to serve his country. And now! The Prime Minster did not know what Lynge knew. He had no knowledge of the decision which the opposition party had made that evening concerning the Ministry, but if it was the fall of the Ministry that they had decided upon, the sun would rise tomorrow over a people who did not know what they had done. The responsibility would be heavy to bear.

Again the Minister apologized for having inconvenienced the editor at this time of night. He had, however, had an idea that his government would be forced to resign soon, perhaps as early as tomorrow.

"Your Excellency may not be mistaken in this," said Lynge. A couple of times, he had wanted to interrupt the Minister to declare that even before he arrived, he had made the decision to let the government remain in its place, but the old parliamentarian had insisted on convincing him, on overcoming his resistance. Lynge let it stand.

The Minister appeared large and magnificent in his armchair. He said amusing things, made graceful gestures, and delivered speeches. With superior art and fervor, he elaborated his opinions on the situation, asked questions, let the other answer, and continued again with fiery words. He respected Lynge's talented resistance and the great sincerity of his attacks. Such attacks could only be based on high and holy conviction and, as such, they did him honor. But now he wanted to ask him, precisely because Lynge was the expert, was the party's unsurpassed talent, if he could defend helping a right-wing government to power now that all the matters the editor, as well as himself and the entire Left Party, had worked for all these years, were finally being resolved. Could he support it?

The Prime Minister always knew what he was saying, and what he meant by his words. He knew Lynge inside out, and nothing about him was hidden from the old and distinguished gentleman. He had followed Lynge's Union-political maneuvers and knew that perhaps he did not have the complete confidence of the Left at all. But the Minister was not blind to this editor's feared and admired journalistic skill. Among the people his name had a great reputation, and his newspaper was widely read and followed. The minister knew that this man could be of use to him. Indeed, he was almost convinced that if Lynge were to put up a bit of a fight on his behalf, his ministry would remain in office despite the secret deliberations that evening.

He rose and offered Lynge a cigar.

The editor was still surrounded by the reverberations of the Minister's eloquence. Yes, he had heard him speak like that before, in the district hall, at public meetings, many years ago. Good heavens, how that man could inspire enthusiasm and virtuous actions!

Lynge said frankly that working to pave the way for a right-wing government was not very appealing to him. He had also considered whether it was at all possible to avoid it. "I have in mind a reconstruction of your Excellency's Ministry."

"Of course!" the minister interrupted quickly. "Of course, we must remove more than half of our councilors and replace them with men who can and will serve their country in this time of crisis."

So they were basically in agreement.

They deliberated for another hour, came to a decision with each other about the details, and thanked each other for each good idea. Only with regard to the newspaper's involvement itself did the Minister wish to leave everything to the editor. He could not write himself. He struck out his hand and said jokingly:

"Your pen, Mr. Editor. It is no pleasure to be subjected to it."

Lynge briefly thought about mentioning the matter with the cross, with the order, which it would naturally be the Minister's pleasure to obtain for him, but it was too petty, too insignificant a matter to bring up on this serious occasion. Lynge decided to wait. There would be other opportunities to mention the order.

At the door, the Minister said as he shook Lynge's hand for the last time:

"I thank you once again for coming. We two have done Norway

a great service today."

And Lynge left.

All the streets were empty. The city had gone to bed. Lynge went up to the editorial office.

He would finish his first article that very evening while his flame was still burning hot. What he would now write would astonish everyone. It would be read aloud, discussed, repeated endlessly, and memorized. He had to do his business well.

Lynge sensed that he was about to add another dent in his political reputation. So what? It would be offset many times over by the great victory he was about to win. He saw in his mind's eye his paper as the largest in the country, with tens of thousands of subscribers, its own telegraph office, its own railroad, branches in all parts of the world, balloons, homing pigeons, its own theater and its own church just for the printing staff. How small it all seemed now in the face of such gigantic visions! And supposing he lost the confidence of some good people? Did it matter? What had he received in return for his endless toil on behalf the nation's heroes? Had it brought him the appreciation he had really coveted? Did the really fine people take off their hats for him? Did the bishop and the general give him a nod? Did their daughters' eyes grow dark with admiration when he passed them in the street? Alas, Alexander Lynge, for all his merits, was ostracized. Even high-minded Leftists began to hold meetings without him. Now there was this daughter of a colonel who had harnessed four horses in Copenhagen—had she pretended to know him when she passed him? Not at all, although he had spoken so favorably of her in his newspaper.

No, one should not play games with him. By God, one should not do that. He was capable of anything. No one knew his full will and power. He would triumph with his new policies, the people would come kneeling to him again, and he would rein them in and bring them to reason. Once again the expectant crowds would await his decisions on all matters.

Lynge stepped into his office. It was dark. He lit a candle and examined the stove. It was empty. Then he sat down at his desk and took up his pen. His article was to be like sword and fire. He dipped his pen to begin, but he stopped.

His eyes fell on the blue letters on the back of his hand, those disfiguring marks that made his hands common. Out of habit and quite mechanically, he began to rub them, blow on them and rub them some more. Then he gave it up.

And Editor Lynge, sitting in the cold room where the fire had gone out, wrote with his marked hands until late into the night.

XIII

For several days, the dispute between Lynge and the Left on the government's reconstruction played out. During these days things had to go as well as possible with the "Tone of the Press." In reality, the tone of the press was not always as it should have been, and when the Right ironically asked the *Gazette* what it had done with its tone, Lynge was silent and did not even bother to reply to this sarcasm. He had other tasks to spend his energies on.

In any case, everything turned out as Lynge had foreseen. The Left was first struck dumb, then the *Northman*'s editor whispered his misgivings, then the *Gazette* replied again, and the battle raged passionately throughout the country. Lynge, by the way, was not without support. He was by no means alone. His supporters within the Left Party of the Parliament and the provincial press extended him a helping hand. The editor of a country newspaper, a man whose honor was so great that no more than half the country doubted it, could not defend letting Lynge fight alone, and he simply went over to the *Gazette*'s opinion and fought along.

Leporello was assigned the task of finding out the mood of the city. He went to the Grand, listened in at the Gravesen, poked his nose into the Ingebret after theater time, and hijacked a parliamentarian on the street, all to find out the city's opinion. And what did the city say? The people either argued about it or were silent. They either participated in the drama or merely observed it. Lynge had by no means succeeded.

Yes, the people resisted. They would not allow him access to victory. Lynge did all he could, and he created so much confusion that for a while the outcome of the battle was uncertain. Meanwhile, his army of supporters had doubled in number. Lynge felt that his pen had done a good deal of splendid work, but wasn't it strange that it did not produce any results? There were no sparks. It was as if all the fire had gone out.

Lynge had written some articles in which he tried to express his unquestionable admiration for the Prime Minister. The words had often been sharper in his paper, and unfortunately, these articles had not always exercised the restraint in their attacks as befitted a paper of the *Gazette*'s high standing, But now there was no time to think about it. Now the Left would seek to unite as one to protect the country from a right-wing government. They would give the Prime Minister another chance, let him try once more, with men who had the confidence of the people, with lovers of the Left's elite. This was the only way out. There was no other option. And Lynge even stated in all seriousness what a foreigner had written to him in jest, that if they just stuck to the government they had in Norway now, they would be doing the right thing, they would be opposing the rebellious revolution in Europe.

The *Northman*'s editor was stubborn and unwilling as usual. He asked if he had heard correctly, if it was really the *Gazette*'s intention to keep this Prime Minister, whom the paper itself had for years and years shamed as a traitor and a liar?

Lynge answered the old fool sarcastically. Although two and two were four, although there was a famine in China, although Emperor Ferdinand was dead, he still insisted on a reconstruction of a liberal Norwegian ministry, rather than letting the Right come to power. Did the *Northman* understand it now?

Inside the halls and out in the corridors of the Parliament, there was the most embarrassing turmoil. The representatives pulled each other around by the buttonholes and confronted each other, full of the most unshakable convictions and full of ulterior motives. If they only knew to whom victory would belong! Which was the right side? They wondered about the election, and did not know whether their poor advice was right or wrong. The old chairman could not give them the slightest clue either. All they could get out of him when he passed by with his head cocked and his hands behind his back was that he unfortunately could not say anything. He did not lean, his heart was pure in that way, but if he had to lean, he almost leaned to both sides.

And Lynge hammered and beat on his iron, made the usual sounds, and swung his hat, but the people did not follow him, and the iron was cold! He had never worked harder. He knew that much was at stake for him, and if he lost here he would pay for it mournfully. It was almost tragic to see this former glory rise up and fight with the fragments of his talent for another former glory. Nothing seemed to help. Day after day, Leporello brought more discouraging news of the mood of the town, and Lynge's spirits sank into a silent rage. What, had they dared to laugh at him in the Grand? Should not the revolution in Europe be stopped?

To add to all this misery, there was also a man who had just come into his office. The man bowed deeply to the editor and said that he was Bondesen, Endre Bondesen.

Yes, the editor knew him. He knew him as a radical and a leftist. Was he not a like-minded man who had his own honest fear of a right-wing ministry?

Bondesen bowed again. Yes, the editor had made no mistake about him, and he was pleased. It was to express his support for Lynge's last policy that he had come. By the way, he had another matter to attend to. He had written a report of a fire in Bernt Ankers Gade, and would the editor be able to use it?

Lynge read through the little article. It was excellent, full of life and excitement. A student had almost been burned to death, having barely saved his life from a window on the third floor. He had come out in his shirt, but with his parents' portrait in his hand. Wasn't it marvelous? And Lynge, who did not know that in this whole lively story, the only truth was the fire itself, was very grateful for this contribution to his newspaper.

Then Bondesen came to his real mission. To his great regret he had learned of a plot against Lynge. An attack was being prepared against him. A pamphlet was already being printed and would probably be published in a day or two. Bondesen was eager to inform the editor of this. It had pained him to see one of the country's most deserving men being dragged down into the dirt by a blackguard. It was shocking.

Lynge listened to this account calmly. Well, what then? Had he not so often been attacked? But a little later he began to realize the danger of a pamphlet being hurled at him at the very moment when his reconstruction policy was hanging in the balance. He asked about the contents, about the nature of the attack. Was it a political pamphlet?

Hardly. It was a shady pamphlet, and Bondesen found it doubly suspicious because it was, of course, being published anonymously.

And did Mr. Bondesen know the author?

Bondesen happily informed him that the author was a Leo Højbro employed in such and such a bank. Perhaps the editor remembered the man who once in the Labour Society meeting had spoken out against the Left and who, among other things, compared himself to a rudderless comet? That man was Højbro.

Lynge remembered him. He had wanted to hate him even then, had made a little fun of the poor speaker, but Mrs. Dagny had defended him. Yes, he remembered him. Back as a mulatto, a bear with heavy limbs, a man who did not read the *Gazette*, was it not so?

Exactly! Bondesen had to admire the editor's memory.

Lynge pondered. But was the brochure personal? Was it not merely a professional attack on his politics?

The pamphlet was also highly personal.

Lynge thought again, his forehead wrinkling as usual when he thought in exasperation. So it had come to this. Pamphlets were being published against him. Was it wise for such a scoundrel to dare to do so? What if Lynge were to stand up to his full lofty height and seek revenge? God save every little worm that lay in his path!

He asked:

"The man's name is Højbro?"

"Leo Højbro."

Lynge noted the name on a piece of paper. Then he looked at Bondesen. So much loyalty, such a fine trait in a man for whom he had never had occasion to do anything good! Lynge was touched. His boyish heart was moved at once, and he asked if he could be of any service to Mr. Bondesen in return. It would be a pleasure to him if he could help him in some way or another later on.

Mr. Bondesen bowed gratefully and asked permission to come again if anything was required. The very first thing he wanted to do was to finish writing his verses, now that he was sure of having them published.

"Yes, if you do, come again. I thank you both for the story of the fire and for your information." Lynge suddenly remembered the Prime Minister's parting words from the other day and added: "You may have done more than me a favor today."

Now Bondesen had only to ask for the necessary discretion. He did not want to be mixed up in what was to come, whatever it might be. Might he hope to remain unnamed?

"Of course, of course, the *Gazette* knows how to maintain its tact." But Lynge suddenly asked, just to be on the safe side, how Bondesen got wind of this secret?

Bondesen replied: By chance, by a lucky coincidence. It was in all respects reliable. He would vouch for every detail with his word.

And Bondesen departed.

Well, well, well! Lynge looked once more at Højbro's name, and hid the paper in a drawer. It was a good thing to know who you were dealing with. It might come in useful one day. People would at any rate admire the *Gazette*'s knowledge of the facts. Yes, there were those who would try to meddle with him, to knock him about. The creepers would not get out of his way. They sat down on their hind legs against him and grumbled! No, his mistake was that he had been too gentle, had been too presumptuous. After this it was to be different!

Ihlen sat in the outer office, wasting ink to no avail. It was only Lynge's pure pity that kept him in his position. But now he had to go. Why the devil should he employ this man any longer, when his redhaired sister now tried to avoid him in the street? Had not the newspaper lost subscribers because of his articles on the Union? Now he was reduced to the most miserable per-column payment, and half of his idiotic reports from the market square and the bazaars were never used. But the man understood nothing. He did not get up and quit. He merely redoubled his efforts in order to earn a little, and there he still sat, growing more and more thin. No, Lynge had been too good to him, and it was to be different from now on.

Lynge resumed his work of reconstructing the Ministry. He was in just the right mood to employ harsh language, and he quickly wrote three pieces as violent, as ruinous, as never before during the whole conflict. Thus the matter was to come to a decision.

That evening, before he left the office, he could keep silent no longer. He called his secretary to him and said:

"There will be a pamphlet published against me soon. I want that pamphlet reported in the *Gazette* just as if it had not been written against me."

The secretary did not really understand this order since the editor would be the first to receive the pamphlet. All mail was brought into his office.

"For one must be above that sort of thing," the editor continued. "One must show humility."

But to explain that his thoughts about this pamphlet which had not yet been published, he added:

"I am afraid that you will probably have to report it during my absence. I may have to go home, go out into the countryside for a few days."

And so the secretary understood his request.

But Lynge had not at all thought of traveling to the countryside. He never actually traveled anywhere.

XIV

In the corridors and committee rooms of the Parliament, the representatives, both Right and Left, were absorbed in the great decision that lay ahead. The most profound seriousness could be read on everyone's faces. Editors, reporters, messengers, notable visitors, and officials mingled among themselves, whispered in corners, shook their heads, held on to their convictions, and were clueless as to their poor advice. Lynge grabbed hold of one, then another of the waverers, trying to convince them of his position. The *Northman*'s editor also strolled about with someone or other at his side. He was shaken, quite pale from the solemnity of the hour. He said almost nothing, and counted the minutes with suspense. Now Vetle Vetlesen had the floor in the hall, but no one cared to listen to him, as his speech was only about the grant for a new lighthouse on the coast. But everyone knew that when Vetle Vetlesen had finished, there would be a disruption. The Right would demand a vote of confidence. The *Northman*'s editor was as reluctant as anyone to see this once-celebrated ministry crumble into rubble in such a despicable manner, but if the Right were to take its place, it could not and should not be denied. For years the government had defied the will of the Left, forced a reactionary church policy, broken promises, and trampled on honesty. It had to fall.

Lynge began to give up hope. He finally inquired with the owner of the factory, Birkeland, but could not move this man of honor a hair's breadth. He shrugged his shoulders, no longer feeling on top of the world. On the contrary, he became tired and bored about the whole affair, and uncomfortable in the midst of this swarm of sad, solemn people who were taking the matter so damned seriously. Lynge could stand it no longer. His nature was revolted by this concern for the country. He did not care to think about it anymore. He stopped the first person he met and made a little joke: "I wonder if Vetlesen will get his lighthouse tonight?" But when the *Northman*'s editor passed by at the same moment, bowed down and crumpled with bitter grief, Lynge was unable to remain composed any longer. He pointed at the editor and said:

"Ah, behold the Lamb of God who bears the burdens of the world!" No, it was impossible to endure this heavy misery! Lynge looked at his watch. He was to meet Mrs. Dagny that evening. They were to go to the theater together at last. It was getting nearer the time, and he did not want to be late as he had been last time. He could do no good here even if he stayed. The outcome was still uncertain, but would it be any more certain if he were present? It would perhaps take another half hour. True, Vetlesen had finally finished his speech, and the representatives poured in to vote, but Lynge could not stay any longer. Neither could he do anything to help.

And so Lynge went to the theater.

Inside the courtroom, the voting was carried out with the utmost deliberation. It was as if everyone was anxious to get it out of their hands and have something new put before them.

Then there was a slight pause.

The gallery was packed with listeners. Leo Højbro had found a seat in the old speaker's box and sat there holding his breath. Every person in the gallery knew what was going to happen and sat motionless.

Then the leader of the Right rose.

"Mr. Chairman!"

The representatives swarmed up to the speaker, formed a ring around him, and stared him in the face. His speech was short and pithy, a question, a question underlined, a demand for an answer.

And when the leader of the Right sat down, the old chairman looked from one to the other, quite troubled by his inclination to lean to both sides. At last, with a paraphrase, he sent the vote of confidence on to its proper addressee, the Prime Minister himself, who was sitting in his seat, fiddling with papers as if no interjection had been made.

The Prime Minister was silent for a moment. Was he now expecting the support that Lynge had worked to scrape together? Why was there no one at his side, not a single one? In former times there was no one who, like him, made the hearts beat and the eyes shine in this hall. Now all was silent. Behind him in the great room he heard only the breathing of the representatives.

His Excellency rose and said a few words. Could one not ride out this storm with a little parliamentary amendment? He made an attempt, said a few words about his long service, and declared that when the country no longer needed him he would find his way home to old age and rest without a pointing finger from the Right. When he sat down he had said many words without a response. His art had been so great.

But the leader of the Right took him to task. Yes or No, an answer, a decision.

And again His Excellency waited a moment. What was he waiting for if none of his supporters dared to be the first to strike a little blow on his behalf? No one rose. No one approached him.

Then the Prime Minister decided the matter. He would hand in his resignation the following day.

And he closed his briefcase on the desk, tucked it under his arm, and left the room, cool and calm, as if no decision had been made. His councilors followed him two by two.

The Ministry had been overthrown.

Højbro forced his way out of his box and finally got out into the corridor with much difficulty. So the present Ministry was gone. Lynge's maneuvers had not been able to save it. What would Lynge's next move be to attract attention?

Højbro had just been in town and sent out his pamphlet. It had not been finished in time to have any influence on the fall of the Ministry, but that was not necessary. Now, however, the stubborn Left had triumphed, and the *Gazette*'s propaganda policy had been beaten back. And Højbro rejoiced in his heart. The Left Party was still on the right path.

He did not regret a single word in his pamphlet. He would not have changed a single sentence. He had portrayed Lynge as a stunted character, a spiritual spokesman with a talent that had been corrupted in his early years and had now sunk down to being a caretaker for a city, a boulevard audience. What did the city say? The townspeople were all laughing yesterday over the Right's disparaging reference to the president of the Parliament. The talk of the town that week was the *Gazette*'s news about the assault in Sandviken. It was a question whether other people in the town had the same pleasure from *Gazette*'s articles as the *Gazette* itself. As soon as anything happened, Lynge came running, bowed, and asked the most honored city for its most honored opinion. And he bowed again when he had heard it.

Well, there was nothing more to be said about that. Nevertheless, this man, without conviction, without integrity, sat in judgment of men and things merely by virtue of his ability to listen to the opinions of the town. His personal looseness dragged down the public discussion, caused confusion wherever he could and weakened the people's sense of responsibility. Lynge will change course, Lynge will make a turn, and Lynge will keep the public in suspense with some strange new thing! He reveals himself from different sides, he surprises, he turns everything stable and fixed upside down. He thinks so little of his own former opinions that he laughs them away loosely and lightly, erases them with a joke and then lets them be forgotten.

To such a man, moral fidelity is but a pleasant domestic virtue, and political fidelity and truthfulness only words. And he acts accordingly. He goes and makes the honest work of the Left uncertain by his sudden maneuvers, strikes at the crooks, fills the press of his brother country with false notions about the Norwegian people and sets us years back in our negotiations with the Swedes about our rights. He does not mean to lay waste to the Left. He merely wants to play his own peculiar tune in the concert to get his newspaper read. He wants a role, to be the talk of the town. Alas, no, he does not want to lay the left-hand side aside. That would be far too crude. He takes the sincerity, the warmest validity from it, and then lets it live on. After he has been a faithful Liberal for three months, and has written in support of his party, he devises a means of astonishing the people in the fourth month, and publishes a column in which he completely upsets the position of the Left and pleases the Right with half-hidden concessions.

In this way Lynge will penetrate the Right. He wants subscribers on the Right. He wants to gain the interest of the Right. And the Right will not show him the door, although not all Right-wingers, not every single one. The polite ones will not let him be thrown out. Will he gain their interest? Well, he is really intriguing, he even makes concessions to them! And the fickle right-wingers, the party's simple-minded wretches, allow themselves to be made fools by this man with his compromises.

Lynge then spreads his imitation honesty over his entire field. The *Gazette* is on the correct side in matters of suicide and moral crimes. The *Gazette* does not let lost spies and agents die quietly with their sins, but exposes them openly and incorruptibly, with cold justice, opens them all to other people's contempt and thereby cleanses society of sin and deception.

But surely there must be something about this man who has created such a deep-rooted reputation as an editor. There was something about him that for a time he was a journalistic force in a country so in need of journalistic forces. And during that time he delivered effective and stirring work. He fired off his epigrams with ferocity. His shots were heard, his shots echoed up among the mountains and down through the valleys, his shots were bold, and no one could equal them. High and low, great and small, all had to accept that they might be a target. Only the most unassailable personalities, the greatest poets, the greatest composers, the greatest sportsmen, these popular heroes of all kinds that the city's opinion protected, only they were safe from Lynge's words. But in this way this man established his position. He attacked horribly, he burned, he branded—yes, but he scandalized those who were worthy of scandal.

And it did not seem to occur to anyone that only in a country where journalism was as poor as in Norway could this man play a role. In a larger country he would have been as insignificant as a pair of scissors in a newspaper office. In Afghanistan he would have climbed up to the village medicine man and done tricks in the sand.

But now the Left had to be wary of this man. As long as the Left was still an unsettled party and was in the midst of the Union negotiations, Lynge would be the Left's for three months and almost the Right's for the fourth. If, on the other hand, the Left were united one day, Lynge would once again belong to the largest party completely and unabashedly. But such disputants should not trouble the pure and ideal cause of the Left. Lynge has shown himself far too much like a gambler. One could expect anything from him, and he was capable of anything. In our public discussion, he has made the seriousness unnecessary and established an exorbitant levity with people and matters that has not yet been seen in Denmark. He was to be regarded as a sharpshooter who came running out of battle and astonished all the ladies of the country by the amount of blood on his clothes. And if the ladies asked him how he was, and how he had fared, he would answer: "How did I fare? I shot ten thousand, then I could do no more. I saw red. But I'll go on again, by God I will—as soon as the prospects are a little better."

This was the content of Højbro's pamphlet. Incidentally, there were also several even more personal things in it, secrets that Højbro could only have learned from Lynge's close circle, from Leporello, from the editor's gallant connections inside and outside the city. On the whole, he had portrayed Lynge with enthusiasm, with a hot temper. This great man who sat in his office and made his judgments about everything and everyone was, in fact, nothing but a rascally boy who was hardly clean under the nose. At the end of his pamphlet, Højbro had declared that his purpose in writing it was to unmask Lynge's journalistic frivolity and chastise his reckless policies. The Left stood no more firmly at a time that it badly needed loyalty and honesty of heart from its people, something which its cause demanded and which it deserved.

Højbro walked homeward with his head spinning. In a week his final installment was due at the bank, and he could not afford it unless a miracle happened. There was no way out. Mrs. Ihlen had spoken to him twice about her inability to repay his loan, and Fredrik was now earning almost nothing at the *Gazette*. He had paid the family's bread bill for the last month, but that was all he had been able to manage. And Mrs. Ihlen had not even seen fit to refuse Højbro when he paid the rent every month. True, she owed Højbro these one and a half hundred crowns, but what was she to do when circumstances were at present so bad for her? The good Mrs. Ihlen was really very much to be pitied, and when Højbro paid her the rent she could not help but accept it. Better days must surely come, she thought. In the worst case, Fredrik might have to try America after all, for so many good people had gone there.

But with all this, Højbro was just as poorly off. He would have to go to the bank manager himself, explain his distress, and ask for a reprieve for this one month. He did not want to explain everything, not to give himself up, but merely obtain another month's respite. Was it not also embarrassing? He had paid all the other installments so far with great punctuality, and now he was stuck on the last one? Another whole month to worry about it. Perhaps in this very month the whole thing might be discovered!

Højbro had arrived home before he even knew it. He opened the front door and met Charlotte coming from the parlor with a dish in her hands. He had not spoken to her for several weeks. She had also become so silent and still. Højbro also noticed that Endre Bondesen no longer came to the Ihlens at all, but he did not make the connection.

He greeted Charlotte, and she replied. She thanked him at once for the pamphlet that he had sent to the house the day before. She had read it with great interest, but Fredrik had shaken his head when saw it. He had also been offended.

She went out into the kitchen with the dish, and Højbro went to his room. He lay back in the rocking chair and half-closed his eyes. How pale and blue she had become. The tiny red spots on her face stood out more clearly, and her lips trembled imperceptibly. Nay, when he remembered the first time he was in the house, how she laughed and beamed then! Now even her voice had become lower, and she looked people in the face with disdain. And yet, still, a flutter of excitement went through him whenever he came near her, and that in spite of her carelessness. She had not even put up her hair.

There was a knock at his door, and he called out: "Come in!"

It was Charlotte again. She had washed and cleaned herself up as in the old days. Her hands were thin and white.

"Excuse me, did I disturb you? I only wanted to ask: did Lynge now know who it was who had written the pamphlet?"

"Perhaps not yet," replied Højbro, "but he will probably find out.

Won't you sit down? Here you are!" And he got up and pulled the rocking chair out for her.

She sat quite still in the chair.

"Then you will be summoned, won't you?" she asked. "I don't know what it's called, but I suppose there will be an interrogation?"

"Do you think so?" he replied, laughing. "You think I've been too mean to the editor?"

Charlotte was silent. Charlotte, who also knew Lynge, did not speak a single word in his defense. She sat upright in her chair, and hardly opened her eyes.

Why, by the way, had she come in to see him just now?

"Mimi Arentzen sends her regards," she said, looking at Højbro with a quick glance.

Højbro had almost forgotten who Mimi Arentzen was. Only after a few questions did he remember that one evening that winter he had accompanied the young lady home in the snow and storm, out of politeness.

"Yes? Thank you!" he said. Well, now he remembered her well. She was strangely beautiful. He remembered her innocent face, it was so fresh and pure, wasn't it? Yes, she had short-cut hair, but . . .

Charlotte leaned down and reached for a loose thread on the carpet.

"Yes, she is beautiful," she said.

"It is strange," he continued, "that this trait of innocence can do so much in essence. One can be ugly, hideous even, but the piercing eyes and the innocent forehead make one beautiful nonetheless, lovable."

Charlotte seized this opportunity to answer:

"Well, that's what they say."

"Yes," he replied, "that's what some people think. Some people are like that. And I am one of them."

There was really nothing more to be said on the subject, but

Charlotte suddenly became uneasy. She exclaimed angrily, vehemently, without being able to restrain herself:

"You have said something of the kind once before, too. In the name of Jesus Christ, why should anyone make such a fuss about innocence. I didn't think you were so medieval, Højbro."

He stared at her in astonishment.

"Medieval? Well, I don't belong to the same brand of Norwegian radicalism as Endre Bondesen, if that's who you got this from. Well, it's not from him? No, no, then it's you and I who don't agree here." A little later he continued: "On the whole, there is no longer any shame in this country to enter into marriage less than pure. The maiden is no more esteemed than the harlot—I beg your pardon! The latter goes as frankly and cheerfully to Karl Johan as any other. Today she openly greets her lover while the whole world looks on and the music plays, and yet tomorrow she goes to the city magistrate with another. I'm just saying that I couldn't marry such a woman. Could I? Knowing that this person to whom you were engaged had been . . . had been . . . sleeping in other beds! All your life knowing that this breast, these arms . . . That one had basically married the leftovers of a human being, and then be condemned to breathe in the scent of another with every breath! But I have said nothing more than that I, for my small part, could not do it."

"Well then, let the one who is so pure have his say," replied Charlotte with a bit of sarcasm.

"I don't understand what it is that has stung you tonight, that you absolutely want to defend such an unfair cause. I don't understand. Pure? You must know that I am not at all pure, but I say what I have said anyway. I am, unfortunately, so little pure that if the world knew what I have done, I might be sitting at this very moment behind bars." Højbro rose excitedly and now stood directly in front of her. "I am not pure at all, and therefore anyone else can say to me: No, I cannot marry you, for you are not pure. It is just as well, I would answer, as I would have done the same thing myself! And then I would either shoot myself, or run away, or try to forget, depending on how deeply I loved."

Charlotte was silent. He said more calmly, with a half smile:

"But—if there should be a pure girl who would marry me in spite of my not being pure myself, well, she feels differently in this matter than I do, and we would marry."

There, now he hadn't deceived anyone, hadn't hidden anything. And why should he even try to embellish himself? His case with Charlotte was lost anyway, quite lost. He had seen that long ago. And even now it was so evident. Charlotte sat there indifferently. Of all he had said she took nothing to heart. Not even what he had revealed about himself had made any impression on her.

"Then you will marry," she said, with an absent look on her face. But she added as she stood up and looked at him: "By the way, I can understand that you are right."

He had not expected this indulgence.

He interrupted hastily, and became angry. "I am not right at all, in general, and I did not mean to say so. But for myself I am right, solely for my own sake. I could not do otherwise."

Then Charlotte went away. She did not say another word, but walked with her head erect, cold and calm as a sleepwalker.

XV

A few days later Højbro left the house to go down to the bank. It was no more than eight o'clock in the morning. It was a mild and clear day, the first sign of spring, and Højbro had taken it into his head to confide in one or other of his comrades about his predicament with the bank. He would certainly be helped if he turned to someone, and the hope of this put him in a happy mood. The morning was bright and clear. A light snow was falling, and the birds were making noises in the trees, hopping from branch to branch and squawking.

He had gone a little way down the street when he saw the Ihlen sisters in front of him, both Sofie and Charlotte. Charlotte had already begun wearing a light jacket.

He almost stopped. He was at once pierced by the uneasiness which always came over him in Charlotte's presence. For a few moments, it was as if he were seated in a swing, half suffocated by the rushing delight that passed through his heart as he sailed downwards. He would have slowed down and stayed behind them all the way, but the ladies had already seen him, and he had no reasonable excuse for turning into a side street. What were the two sisters doing in the street so early in the morning?

They greeted each other, and Sofie mentioned at once that it was the beautiful weather that had lured them out. Charlotte was remarkably pleasant to look at. She no longer hung her head. If the occasional passerby they met happened to stare at her a little because she looked so fine today, she laughed aloud and made witty remarks

"You ladies should take the opportunity to visit the exhibition at nine o'clock," he said.

Sofie was willing. What did Charlotte think?

Charlotte quickly said "No."

No, no, Højbro also said, then they should go to the Parliament. It was also very interesting there nowadays. But Charlotte did not want to go to the Parliament either. Charlotte wanted to walk the streets and see people.

Well, then, there was nothing to be done about it. When everything he proposed was rejected, he would say no more. Højbro was silent.

"Are you very much looking forward to the spring?" asked Sofie.

"Yes, I am. I don't know that I have ever longed for it more than I do this year," he replied.

"That is quite true," remarked Charlotte, and laughed shortly. "I don't suppose there has ever been a winter as cold as this past one."

Sophie gave her sister a surprised look.

They had walked as far as the park. Suddenly Sophie stopped and said, annoyed:

"I have forgotten my book. Now I must go back."

"Mr. Højbro can do that," said Charlotte, pointing to Højbro with her head.

Sofie gave her another glance.

"I put the book on the table but, of course, I forgot it," she said.

"Yes, but Højbro can fetch it," said Charlotte again. She said it with a firmly furrowed brow.

"One must first ask Mr. Højbro if he would be so kind," said Sofie.

"With pleasure," he had to answer. "What kind of book is it? Where is it lying?"

"It is lying in plain sight. It is a book that needs to be returned to the lending library. But it is wrong to trouble you."

"Let him go," interrupted Charlotte.

And Højbro left.

When he returned, the sisters were still loitering in the same place.

"How quick you were. Thank you so much!" said Sofie. She was very grateful for this favor.

They continued walking.

"It will soon be time for cycling again," said Sophie to her sister.

"I'll never ride again," replied Charlotte. "You can borrow the bicycle for a year if you like."

"That's the gratitude one has," said Sophie jokingly to Højbro. "No sooner has she gotten the bicycle than she throws it away again."

"I'll give it to you!" Charlotte said fiercely and firmly.

"Well, that's even better! " Sofie tried to brush it off, but her sister's irritable mood annoyed and embarrassed her. "Shame on you!" she said softly.

Suddenly Charlotte's face turned pale, and she exclaimed:

"You are really intolerable, Sofie. When I said that Mr. Højbro would probably fetch the book, that was wrong. If I say that now you can use the cycle for a year instead of me, I know that Mr. Højbro won't mind. But immediately that is wrong too. I can do or say nothing without it being wrong."

There was a pause. Sofie was searching for something to say.

"All that is needed now is for Mr. Højbro to begin to reprimand me," Charlotte continued.

"Me?" replied Højbro. "What should I have to reprimand you for?"

"I merely said that it was all that was needed."

They had walked down as far as the university clock, and Højbro said:

"Shall we go into the Grand and have a drink? I have a little time for it."

"Thank you," Charlotte replied, "but we are going to the library, this way," and she pointed down towards Tivoli Gardens. "But thank you very much anyway."

She had answered more graciously than at any other time during the entire walk. He suspected that it was his clothes that were to blame for her not wanting to go with him to the Grand. He had no overcoat as yet, and even his jacket was beginning to unravel at the edges. He said with a slightly bitter smile:

"Very well then. I will go to the Grand myself for a moment and get something to warm me. It is true what Miss Charlotte says. I am a little cold."

He wanted to take his hat and disappear but Charlotte at once held out her hand to him. He was quite astonished. She squeezed his hand before she and Sophie walked on, and as he walked down the street he wondered why she had suddenly done so. Did she really want to condescend to be amiable now, just to wipe out the impression of her cruelty all morning? He had held her hand in his only a few times before. He still felt the happy, rippling movement in his breast, and heard her voice when she said, "You are warm, aren't you? I feel your warmth through my glove. You are not cold, are you? It was in winter."

But what did it all mean? Why had she been downright rude when he had done nothing to her? And she would even give away the bicycle. Well, now it was just one more bond that had been broken. Why on earth was he still concerned about her?

He watched her. She walked through the college garden, and her light jacket fitted her so wonderfully. She looked like a butterfly among the trees. But in God's name, let her go, let her flutter away, disappear! Now he was more distant from her than ever. She had been cruel to him all morning.

He stopped. There—there she disappeared! And Højbro stared for a moment longer at the thicket which had hidden her. He wrung his hands silently and fiercely. No, she did not appear again. Then he moved on.

When he came to the Grand, he thought at first of passing it by, for he didn't really have the heart to drink coffee. But when he remembered that he had said he would go there after all, he wanted to keep his word. And it would not cost very much either.

He had his coffee and sat down to consider which of his comrades he could approach about his deadline with the bank. He was looking for a man who was good for forty or fifty crowns. It would be unlikely that he would not find such a man. Suddenly there was someone beside him who said good morning.

It was Endre Bondesen. He was wearing a fine new suit, and his face was full of joy.

Bondesen had discovered a brand new way of raising money. After the unhappy showdown with Charlotte, he had decided to change his residence in order to make his address unknown. No one could know whether the girl might not think of something, and perhaps come back one day. Nor had he rented in Parkvejen for any length of time, and when the month was up he moved into a two-room apartment in Bernt Ankers Gade. He had been there only a few days when a small harmless kitchen fire broke out on the floor below. The fire was immediately extinguished and nothing of value was destroyed. The occupants went to bed and slept peacefully until morning as if nothing had happened. Only Bondesen did not sleep. He was embarrassed. He was short of money, and he devised the most ingenious plans to get some. What if he took advantage of the fire? Should he not consider this little incident with the fire as a happy coincidence that came to his aid? He himself brought a little lively written report to the *Gazette*, giving an account of the details: In the fire, there was no one else who suffered loss but a student who was mentioned only by his initials. He lost all of his belongings, his books, and his clothes disappeared in the flames. The student had his parents' picture in his hands when he threw himself out of the window.

That edition of the *Gazette* had brought the matter to his father's attention. It was, by the way, Bondesen's firm hope that a sum of such and such a size might help him to get back on his feet. So far he had acquired some clothes on credit, so he was not entirely naked.

And this appeal to his father had the desired effect. In particular, the story of photograph that was carried out of the fire had moved the old man in Bergen very much. He had stretched himself further than he really had the means to, had sold a little of his livestock, borrowed a little from a neighbor, and scraped together a great deal of money. From that day on, not only was Endre able to pay off all of his debts here and there, but also to take ladies to the carnival all winter long. Moreover, he was able to purchase many fine clothes. Now Endre Bondesen was in high spirits again, and was cheerful and radiant.

"Yes," he said to Højbro, "here you can see! I haven't slept for three nights, it's true, but does it bother me? Is it only skin and bones. But I have the bicycle to thank for that. You don't know how the wheel strengthens a man. Yes, sorry, but if you had a bicycle yourself, you wouldn't be so pale-faced."

And Højbro, this bear who could bring Bodensen to his knees with one hand, made no objection to this.

"Well, of course, one does succumb eventually," continued Bondesen, "when one does not sleep for three nights. But then we all die at some point. By the way, have you seen the *Gazette* today? Lynge mentioned the pamphlet. Here it is on the very first page."

Højbro took the paper and read the little notice. It was as reasonable as it could be. Only at the end the usual snarl that made its mark: The author had made an attempt to disgrace well-known men who had served the community for many years, and the *Gazette* and its editor were above such contemptible anonymous attacks. Nor was anything secret to the *Gazette*. It knew the identity of the slanderer, a man whose reputation was questionable.

Højbro bit his lip. Whose reputation questionable! And for the *Gazette* nothing was secret! Hm.

"Well," said Bondesen, "the issue is probably not settled with this. I'm certain it will be taken up again."

"Yes," Højbro replied. "If I know Lynge right, he will probably raise this matter again."

"Which is perfectly reasonable. Yes, I remember your opinion of Lynge. It is not the best."

"In reality, it is no worse than if the author of the brochure went to Lynge and said: Here I am now, it is I who have attacked you, and I have come here to tell you so. If the man did that, Lynge would feel appeased by this attention towards him and would welcome it. "

"I can see that you are in complete agreement with the author of the pamphlet."

"Yes, I agree with him completely."

Pause.

"Do you know the author?"

"Yes, I do."

"Dare I ask who it is?"

"It is me."

Bondesen had not expected this answer. He stared for a moment at Højbro and was silent. There was again a pause.

"Take a look at the verses on the next page at once," said Bondesen.

So, Bondesen had finally made his debut. It was a hymn to spring, three verses, great, mighty lines, a fresh cheer for the budding and blossoming in the people and the Fatherland. Every new beginning was for the good.

Bondesen had really taken great pains with these lines and put a lot of feeling into them.

"What do you think?" he asked.

"I congratulate you!" replied Højbro. "It is well done, I think. I have no great appreciation for poetry but..."

"Really? We must have a drink to that," cried Bondesen, and knocked on the table.

But now Højbro got up. He had to get to the bank if he was not to be late. He had only five minutes left.

And so he left.

So, Lynge had him in the palm of his hand now. He knew what to expect. Lynge was not the sort of man who would spare him. If that man walked against a wall in the dark, he would strike his fist against the wall in exasperation, and once more he would grit his teeth and strike his fist against the wall to give vent to his boyish rage. But he could forgive if he was asked to. He was no worse than that.

But did he really know anything? Where could he have learned anything? From the bank manager? In that case, Højbro would have been suspended immediately. Was it really out of sheer impudence that Lynge threw out this information about his place of work? When he got to the bank he would no doubt get it cleared up.

Højbro, as usual, stepped through the double glass doors. He saluted, and the staff answered. He saw nothing unusual in their faces. When the manager came in, he too returned his greeting without displaying any suspicious expression. Højbro could not understand it.

Hour after hour passed, and nothing happened. When the manager was about to leave the bank, he politely called Højbro into his office. Now—now, indeed! Højbro calmly laid down his pen and stepped into the manager's office. Of course, now he was to get the sting. "I just wanted to ask you a question, if you'll allow me," said his boss. "I have been informed that you are the author of a pamphlet that was published a few days ago."

"Yes," replied Højbro.

Pause.

"Have you read today's *Gazette*?" continued the manager.

"Yes, I have."

Again a pause.

"I hope you have such a high regard for yourself that you completely ignore what the paper has written about you, and that you do not take any action in that respect. Your statement was a good one."

Højbro's lips began to tremble. He would have understood it if he had been dismissed from his post, chased away, and arrested in front of the manager's eyes. This thoroughly honest man had been like a father to him for ten years. He knew nothing. Højbro just said:

"I thank you, Mr. Director. Thank you. Thank you. Thank you!"

The bear cried.

The manager looked at him, nodded, and said briefly:

"Yes, that was all, Højbro. You may go."

And Højbro, in his agitation, was moved to thank him again, and he left.

He stood at his desk until closing time, full of thoughts, quite dumbfounded. Did Lynge really know anything? If he knew the slightest thing, he would bring him down abruptly, without further notice, as soon as tomorrow as any other day. The whole day had been so full of uneasiness and surprises: first Charlotte's premonitions in the morning, then her hand pressure which was still with him in his innermost being, and finally the boss's kindness, which affected him more than anything else, yes, more than anything else. If only he did not have to drag the old man of honor out of his delusion!

When he came home in the evening he lighted his lamp, locked his door, and sat down in the rocking chair without doing anything. Half an hour later there was a knock at his door, but he did not get up to open it. There was another knock, but he still did not open the door. Instead, he blew out the lamp and remained motionless in his chair. God help him if it was Charlotte! He was not able to see her now. She had probably read the *Gazette*, too, and made up her mind. What would he say to her? But it certainly couldn't be Charlotte, and if it was, she might just hate him a little again. It wasn't impossible. What did he know?

The knocking ceased. He sat there in the chair, fell asleep, and woke up late at night in the dark, frozen, dead in feet and arms, with a head still swirling with dreams. He wondered what time it was.

He went to the window and drew aside the curtain. Moonlight, mild weather, silence. A messenger came walking up the street. It was the only living thing he saw. In the glow of the gas lamps, he noticed that the messenger had a red full beard and a leather hat. Well, what if this man had a beard or not? He decided it was best to undress and get into bed.

Suddenly he stopped and stood still. He heard a faint noise below. Something was being rolled, something was being pulled. He went to the window again, and saw that the messenger had stopped right down below, outside the front door. What was going on, what was being rolled? He opened the window a little and looked down. The bicycle emerged from the door, slowly, cautiously, led by Charlotte. The messenger stood right beside her and helped. Then Charlotte let go, and she said something, said in a low voice a name, an address, and asked the messenger to come back in the morning with the money he would get.

Højbro knew this address very well. The bicycle was going to the pawnbroker, the same place in the town where his own affairs were also settled.

XVI

In the *Gazette* office things had begun to quiet down. Lynge's numerous views on politics had made his friends shy away. Only one or two of the most faithful, people who had banded together to form an alternative party—a lawyer, a couple of professors, three or four politicizing women—still visited him regularly and spoke moderately to the public through his newspaper. No one knew anymore where Lynge himself truly stood on political issues.

He hardly knew himself. In his office, buried in newspapers and documents, brooding, disappointed and defeated, Lynge sat in his chair and pondered. His chair had once been like a throne, but now it could hardly be considered a solid stool, and he himself had sunk down to the level of a downright bad editor among other editors who are caught in errors, in wavering, even in cheating. So many things, so many things can happen in the world!

The last few days had been hard for Lynge. He had even been rejected by Mrs. Dagny on their evening at the theater. He had been turned down, and had almost been put out of the door by the beautiful woman. He had never before ventured so far forward without being sure of victory, and now his warm heart had run away with him and led him into trouble with the coldest, most calculating coastal town lady! He could hardly believe it. True, he had not been able to do Mrs. Dagny the pleasure of giving her the cross. Circumstances had been against him. The Ministry had fallen, and the opportunity was gone. But he had hoped that Mrs. Dagny would find something in himself, in his person, that she could appreciate. It turned out that this little cross was really of great importance to this woman, and that if the cross could not be obtained, it was all over between her and him. Wasn't that ridiculous? He had hardly touched her at all. He had grasped her by the waist and giggled inwardly as he was wont to do: "Tee-hee, you're mine, you are!" But then she had gone away at once into her bedroom, where she locked the door behind her. She left it to old Miss Gude to see him out. That was the sad end of the visit.

For several nights Lynge had again slept with clenched fists, just as in his first days as a student, when he had offered himself to many employers and been rejected everywhere. He was beginning to feel the horrors, and Højbro's pamphlet had also caused him a great deal of trouble and thought, from which he had previously been free. What was he to do with this libel? Scorn it, make a joke of the whole thing? Now there was no longer any Mrs. Dagny to pray for the fool, the rudderless comet. It must be possible to mock him to pieces on the spot, and bury him in the laughter of the people. On the other hand, was it advisable to play along with this man, to challenge him so boldly? God knows what he might do. One might expect anything from such a scoundrel. Lynge resolved to keep quiet about both the writing and its author. It was the noblest thing to do. And he certainly knew that if he kept silent, the other papers would also keep silent, right up to the *Northman*, who would wait three weeks before saying whatever was to be said, and who would collectively bury the matter forever.

But when two weeks had passed, it was impossible for Lynge to keep this resolution. He could no longer remain idle. It was not in his nature. He must at least assert the *Gazette*'s reputation as the best-informed paper and tell the world that the anonymous slanderer was known. The man worked in such and such a bank, his reputation was perhaps not to be questioned, Lynge knew nothing about that, but he would venture a slight hint in the direction of a guilty deed. A man who was denounced by his own friends must have something to answer for, and Endre Bondesen had expressly called him a scoundrel and a simpleton. For safety's sake, Lynge sent the exasperated Leporello down to Højbro's boss to inquire, but Leporello was shown the door. Then Lynge found that things were beginning to go beyond all bounds. Was the *Gazette*'s man, his man, shown the door? His boldness flared up, and he went down to the bank manager himself, in the name of law and order. He still has his old strength in him, and he entered the bank with his head held high, like a man who never bows, never gives an inch. He told the manager in private his errand—the books out! But the door was just as politely, just as gracefully opened for him, and when he was outside, the door was closed again!

Lynge's patience was gone. He went up to his office and wrote his first preliminary notice with his eyes blazing.

Højbro's pamphlet was really so unfair, so one-sided, that it could explain Lynge's indignation. Alas, how one-sided it was! A man with his great merits and good heart should not be the laughingstock of the country, even if he, in times when the news was scarce, had changed positions in politics to bring his newspaper into the spotlight. In the midst of his adversity, Lynge also had an eye and ear for others than himself. Had he perhaps completely neglected the poor poet in the attic in Tordenskjoldsgaden? Lynge had not forgotten him. Until now Fredrik Ihlen had occupied a chair in the *Gazette*'s office, but now he was finally going away. Lynge had found another man to take his place, the new, promising genius of Tordenskjoldsgaden. Lynge had read the novel he had begun and found it very admirable. One could not let such talent go to waste. One had to support talent. And at the thought of this, Lynge's heart was once again open, and he again showed his marvelous ability to bring talents to their full potential.

He opened the door and called out:

"Ah, Ihlen, may I speak to you for a moment?"

And Ihlen entered Lynge's office.

"We have decided in a meeting today to lighten our budget a little," he said. "I have thought that I might be able to manage with a little less help in the editorial department, and there may be no other solution than for the two of us to part."

Ihlen stared at him. His face had lately grown long and pale. For weeks he had toiled like a slave to pay his mother's bakery bill. The paltry payment Lynge had reduced him to had driven him to write scraps and notes night and day, innumerable notes, which Lynge, at intervals of a few days, read through and discarded. If he was in a partcularly good mood he might pick out a few of these poor papers and toss them to the printer with an indulgent smile. Ihlen could not understand why his work had suddenly become so bad, and he wrote and crossed out, torturing himself to the utmost to do better next time. And all to no avail. His pieces were returned to him, in whole bundles, and on the previous day without even having been read.

"We will of course be pleased to receive contributions from you," the editor continued when Ihlen fell silent. "But we must terminate your position at the paper."

"But why is that?" Ihlen finally asked, and he stared quite puzzled at the editor in his simplicity.

"Yes, why? It is, after all, a decision, and besides . . . But you don't have to go today. It can be tomorrow or another day."

But Ihlen still didn't understand.

"I don't think this is really very considerate," he said.

In the face of so much naïveté, Lynge just shrugged his shoulders and replied:

"Considerate? Well, that's how different opinions can be. Have we not already printed quite a few of your works and paid you well for them? You can't complain about inconsideration, can you? If I remember correctly, we even published a story about your mother's needlework once and tried to get her some employment."

"Well, that has nothing to do with this situation," Ihlen answered.

Lynge grew impatient. He sat down in his chair and reached for some papers which he looked through.

Now Ihlen's honest indignation arose. Was he not a grown man, and had not the *Gazette* itself made a name for him in the field of domestic science? He said:

"I really haven't earned so very much lately that even this little bit should now be taken away from me."

"But my God, man," replied Lynge angrily, "haven't you realized already that we can't use what you write? You ought to be able to see for yourself that it is useless. It is of no interest. No one reads it."

"But you yourself once said that it was good."

"Ah well, one can never be too careful in issuing such testimonials."

There was nothing more for Ihlen to do. He kept silent and retreated backwards out of the door. And the scholarship? Hadn't Lynge also promised him a scholarship in due course?

Ihlen went into the back office. The secretary asked:

"Something going on?"

"Dismissed," Ihlen replied with a pale smile.

He began to gather up his papers and clear his desk, pulling out his bundles of discarded manuscript notes from drawers and shelves. He wanted to take them all with him, especially the manuscript of his first famous article on the varieties of berries, the great national question of two million, which still lay among his papers as a dear reminder of his glory days. And when he had finished he wanted to see the editor and say goodbye, but he had to wait a moment. A man had just come in, Kongsvold, Lynge's old acquaintance from his student days and member of the Ministry, who walked straight into the editor's office as if his business could not be delayed.

Lynge welcomed him with a questioning look. "There you are! Please, sit down!"

Kongsvold looked secretively around, thanked him in a low voice, and took a piece of paper from his pocket.

"It is the list," he said, "the nominations for the jury members. It goes to Stockholm this evening."

At this unexpected surprise, Lynge's gratitude rose high. He perused the list, swallowed it with his curious eyes, and shook Kongsvold's hand.

"You have done me a great favor, old friend. You may be sure that I shall remember it."

But Kongsvold dared not hand over the list for fear that his handwriting might betray him. One could never know what might happen. There might be questions about its source. Lynge must copy the list himself.

"I hope, for God's sake, that you will not betray me!" said Kongsvold.

"What are you saying? You don't for a moment think anything so bad about me, do you?"

"No, no, I am just so frightened. No, of course you wouldn't give me away voluntarily, but I meant involuntarily, unwittingly. And what would happen if you were put under pressure?"

"I am never pressed any further than I want to be, Kongsvold. Of course, I will never reveal your name. I am no traitor."

Then Kongsvold got up to leave.

"Well," said Lynge, "now you've got a right-wing boss again? Yes, that's how it turned out."

And Lynge nodded:

"And what was it I had said? A government that breaks faith and laws will not last forever in Norway. That is how far we have come."

The two men look at each other. Lynge did not blink.

"Farewell," Kongsvold said.

But Lynge didn't want him to leave.

"Wait a moment and I'll go with you. We'll go to the Grand. "

"No, I dare not. People must not see us together. Not now."

And Kongsvold left.

When Ihlen came into Lynge's office to say goodbye, he encountered a completely different man. The editor was quite cheerful. Lynge said:

"I will give you an account of what you are owed. The cashier has gone now, but you can see him tomorrow."

"I have nothing more due from you," replied Ihlen, "I have received the last of it."

"Yes, yes. Well, send us an article or two when you feel like it."

Then Ihlen said goodbye and left.

No one stopped him in the streets. People recognized him and let him calmly walk by with the pile of discarded notes under his arm. Ihlen had served his time, he had satisfied the people's curiosity and was done. Now it was time for the next person.

Ihlen arrived home without a single person tipping their hat to him.

XVII

When Højbro came home in the evening, he was met in the hall by Mrs. Ihlen, who in a very downcast and mournful voice told him what had happened to Fredrik. Now he had no alternative but to try America. If he sold his books and his desk he might perhaps get enough to pay for the journey. At any rate, he could not go to any of his family. He would certainly have refused to do so, nor, perhaps, would it have done any good. Ever since Fredrik had become an employee of the *Gazette*, all the Ihlens had shown him the greatest coldness. Incidentally, the lady was now so fortunate as to be able to pay back Højbro the loan, those one and a half hundred crowns. It was long overdue and she had to apologize.

But could she afford this money now, when such severe changes in the family were impending?

Yes, she had been given this money for that very purpose. It was Charlotte who had given it to her. Charlotte had had it saved up. Poor Charlotte, she was so good! As soon as she heard that her mother owed Højbro money she immediately said: It shall not happen, not a day longer! Now she had gotten her way. God knows what had become of Charlotte. She had gone through so much this winter. She had never said anything, but her mother had understood. Mrs. Ihlen had not been blind. Many weeks ago Endre Bondesen had stopped coming to the house, and that must have been of some significance. Something had certainly happened. But it hurt her so bitterly. Charlotte had thrown her arms around her mother's neck and said that she would have gone to America if only she had had the money, but she had none.

Mrs. Ihlen told him all this in a low and confidential voice, so as not to be heard by the girls in the parlor. Then she gave him the money she had in her hand. Højbro knew very well where this money had come from. It was the loan on the bicycle. He objected. He would not accept this money now. Charlotte must keep it for the present. She could use it for traveling money. But Mrs. Ihlen shook her head.

No, she had been ordered to give him the money. Charlotte would simply turn her back if she tried to return it to her. Here you are!

Højbro rushed into his room and threw himself forcefully into the rocking chair. Thank God, now he could settle his affairs with the bank! He could draw out the papers tomorrow morning at nine o'clock, before the manager arrived. And so he had only one night left, one night only, and during this night he would sleep as happily as any man could.

How he had suffered during the winter, with no salvation in sight! He had written this pamphlet, which had been sold to one and then to another, but Højbro had made no profit from it. He had given the manuscript away to the first printer who would accept it and was glad to be able to have it published without expense. So the days went on and the deadline drew nearer and nearer.

And he had just come home that evening to think it over once more, to sit down in this same rocking chair, and to really think hard of ways of obtaining the money he needed. He had asked a couple of his friends for help but it had been in vain. He would have sat here in this very spot, without lighting the lamp, just as now, and thought about it for many hours. And now he sat here with the money in his hand!

The two large notes smelled a little musky and they crackled between his fingers. He was not mistaken, he had them. Was it not wonderful? He could not sit still. He stood up in his dark room and smiled. When he heard footsteps in the hall he quickly opened the door and looked out. Normally, he would have sat still and held his breath while he listened. But this time he opened the door with a cheerful jerk, utterly without hesitation.

"Good evening!"

"Good evening, Miss Charlotte!" he replied, and stood there in the doorway.

"Are you going out so late?" she asked.

"Out? No, I'm not. I just thought it was your brother coming, and I wanted to say good night."

"My brother is in the parlor," she said. "Shall I fetch him?"

"No, not at all. I just wanted to . . . It was nothing, nothing at all."

They stood there facing each other. She looked past him into his dark room and asked:

"Have you not lit your lamp this evening?"

"Yes, my lamp? I shall light it at once."

He motioned with his eyes to the money lying on his table, but she interrupted him:

"I beg your pardon for being so rude the last time we met."

Well, surely, that was nothing to apologize for. And besides, perhaps he himself was guilty of the same. He replied:

"You can be however you like with me, you know. Besides, you were no different last time than usual . . . yes, I mean . . ."

"I hope so," she interrupted, laughing. And she added, quite seriously: "I don't know why, but I was so irritable, almost sick with spite. Did you understand that?"

"No, I didn't."

"Yes, I was. But I never will be that way again, Højbro. I would have asked you to forgive me that very evening, but when I knocked at your door but you did not answer."

"So it was you after all! Yes, I suspected it, but I dared not see you then. I could not look you in the eye."

"No?"

"No. But you couldn't understand that, could you?"

"Oh yes, I can understand that. One may indeed have committed some secret sin that one must turn a blind eye to." She wanted to show that she was with him, that she could understand and apologize.

He took this as an invitation to continue. He made up his mind to tell her what his sin was, a fraud, a forgery. He once lacked money for a bet he had lost, truly, a bet on his word of honor, and then he produced false documents and got the money.

He began:

"It went like this..."

But she interrupted him again:

"No, no, no. You mustn't tell me anything! We won't tell each other anything, will we? No, dear, let us be a little merry tonight, or things might go so wrong with me. I can hardly stand it any longer." She tried hard not to burst into tears.

He was too puzzled to go on. He did not say a word. For a moment he thought again of thanking her for the money but it was perhaps it would too much for her to remind her so directly of her mother's poverty, the pawnbroker, the bicycle, and so he remained silent.

Then she began to ask him about the old portraits on his table, about his parents, about his only sister, all these things she had never mentioned before. And she was delighted when he showed her a picture of his sister.

"You are so kind this evening," he said. "May I also show you my last letter from home? But the spelling is not quite right everywhere."

She took the letter and read it with downright enjoyment. What wholesome and firm sentiments. What love! They were both amused at the end, where his old father, who hardly ever joked, had written the letters of the alphabet, one after the other, and added: "Enclosed herewith are a few characters which you must put here and there in the letter yourself to correct my mistakes."

Charlotte sat looking at Højbro while he put the letter away again.

They began to talk about Fredrik. He had made up his mind to try his luck in America, and had already begun to sell his books. It appeared that he now had enough to pay for his ticket. Charlotte said she would have followed him if she had the means to do so. She told him, with a smile that was almost a sigh, that she had been praying to God all afternoon for traveling money—as unworthy as she was of his help.

"No, you must not," said Højbro carelessly. "You must not go."

"Why shouldn't I? Yes, I would so much like to. I am so tired of myself here."

"But there is no one else who is tired of you. Many people would miss you very much if you left."

"Who would miss me?"

He himself most, he himself nights and days, he thought. But he answered: "Since you ask, Endre Bondesen, for one."

"No," she cried in a hoarse voice, clenching her fist. "I do not wish to be missed by him, not even to be remembered." She changed her tone, and said, "We should be happy tonight, shouldn't we?"

"Yes, let us," he replied.

However, she herself could not forget the matter of Endre Bondesen. She began to talk about him again. He had made her as unhappy as one person could make another unhappy. Well, now they should not talk about him anymore and just be happy.

"But you must have loved him once," said Højbro, "and then..."

"Now I will tell you something, but you won't believe me. You won't. I have never loved him. I am as sure of that now as I am sure that I am sitting here. I hope that you understand what I am saying, but I suppose you don't. I have never loved him. I had only been infatuated with him for one evening. And I have known all the time since that night that I did not love him, but I have tried to convince myself that I did. Yes, I wanted to do it. God only knows why."

Højbro felt an intense joy. His face flushed, and he did not attempt to conceal it. Yes, that was how it was: one man's loss was another man's gain. In the midst of his curious and happy excitement he wanted to go on talking, to know more, but she reached out her hand towards him, touched his hair with her fingers, and said with a beseeching look:

"Yes, but, my dear, let us talk of something else!"

She had unintentionally stroked his hair when she withdrew her hand. The blood rushed in his veins from head to foot, and he took her hand, and held it.

"But I shall miss you too if you go away," he said, close to her ear.

"Yes, perhaps you will," she said just as softly. "But you must know that I am not worthy of it."

"Oh, but you are!"

He drew closer to her, knelt down by her chair, and took both her hands. She let him keep them, and she whispered with a smile:

"We mustn't be doing this. Someone might come."

"No, there are no sounds. No one is coming. I am as happy at this moment as never before in my life, never. Look, I am holding your hands here, do you see that?"

"Yes, I do."

Then there were footsteps in the hall, and somebody crossed the floor and went into the kitchen. Charlotte stood up startled, but immediately sat down again. Højbro took her hands again and kissed them. He patted her thin, white hands which he had so often kissed in his dreams. Now he put his lips to them in warm delight. And he spoke, whispered a few words, hoping that it was not all a dream, prayed that he might really be allowed to be fond of her now as he had been fond of her all the time. No one, no one had known how his heart had longed for her all this winter.

She replied:

"You say you are happy now, Højbro, but you will not say that tomorrow."

"Tomorrow and always, if I may! You are the only one who makes a fuss about it. Why not tomorrow? Precisely tomorrow, especially tomorrow. For tomorrow I will be settling an unpleasant matter that has been troubling me for a long while, and if I am able to see you tomorrow evening I will ask you something, ask you on my knees for something, Charlotte."

Charlotte suddenly rose to her feet and shielded herself with both hands:

"No, no, we mustn't do any more, for God's sake! Now I must go. Thank you, thank you for tonight! And Højbro, you must not ask me for anything on your knees. Good God, I will answer you 'No,' absolutely. You must not do it, do you hear? I must go now."

"Will you answer me 'No'? I have held your hands, I have kissed them, but you will still say 'No'? Will you never say 'Yes'? Give me a little hope. Put me to the test. Give me a long time to wait. I can wait a long time as long as I have hope."

The footsteps sounded again in the hall, No one had seen anything. Then the footsteps died away in the parlor, and all was silent.

Charlotte already had her hand on the doorknob. She was flushed, her chest heaving.

"I love you," she said calmly. "Yes, it is you I love, but I say must say 'No.'"

They looked at each other.

"You love me! Yes, do you? Do you really? Dear, but then you mustn't say 'No,' not forever? Why, why, tell me?"

She stepped quickly up to him, took his head between her hands, and kissed him right on the mouth. She whimpered once, excitedly, as she did so. Then she put her arm up in front of her face and ran to the door.

He called after her, no longer observing any caution, but came straight to the door and called out:

"Why, Charlotte, why do you say that?"

"Because," she answered in a dry whisper, "because I am no longer a pure woman. I am not pure, no."

She still kept her arm in front of her face to hide herself. Then she took a few steps across the floor, opened the door, and disappeared.

Højbro closed his door and remained standing in the middle of the room. Not pure? What did that mean? Was Charlotte not pure?

She had kissed him, she really had. He still felt it. And why had she said she wasn't pure? This purity thing was his own old, stupid idea.

But in Heaven's name, was Charlotte not pure? Well, what if she wasn't? She had kissed him. She loved him. How was it, had she not told him straight out that she loved him? But she was not pure, she had then said, and it did not matter if she loved him. Who was pure? He himself was not pure. He was even a criminal, a perpetrator, and he would not be able to pay off his debt until tomorrow.

He looked at the money on the table, and the large notes lay in their place. Tomorrow he would go to Charlotte with his great yearning. Wasn't she pure? Oh, purer than he, purer than anybody. He would really kneel before her. And she loved him. She had kissed him!

He was overwhelmed by this recollection, pierced by wild delight, and he stood there in the middle of the floor without doing anything. She had worn her dressing gown, a thin dress through which you could see her corset, and her arms were bare almost to the elbow, so short were the sleeves. How strangely sweet they were, too. But what if someone else had kissed those arms before? Well, what then? Of course, others had kissed them. She herself said she was not pure. Those same arms had probably even rested on other people's necks. But she was pure enough. He loved her.

The lamp burned softly on the table, and the glow from its dome was steady and burned as if no one, nothing could stand in his way.

He sat down in the rocking chair. But those arms had already rested on others. Could that be forgotten? They would embrace him as they had embraced others. They could never be just his. She could make comparisons between his embraces and those of others.

Deeper and deeper he sank into thought. No, was she really not pure? He remembered that he had met her outside Bondesen's door, that he had bumped into the two of them in corridors and in secluded places. She who he had worshipped every day and hour since the first time he saw her! She would come to him full of experience, accustomed to anything, would be tender to him as to others, and embrace him with her practiced arms. And then he would go through life knowing that this was so! He could not do it. No, it was impossible.

The lamp burned on.

Hour after hour passed, first in rapture that Charlotte loved him, then in despair. He beat his head. No, it was impossible, and he knew it so well that he could not bear it. She could have stolen, murdered—anything but this. Then the lamp burned dry, and when it began to sputter he blew it out. He lay back on his bed fully dressed and with wide-open eyes. Charlotte's kiss still burned on his mouth. To think that she had prayed to God for traveling money! She was not depraved, and he loved her very much. But what was the use?

It was only when morning came and his curtain could no longer keep out the light that his eyes became leaden and he drifted away, slipped into a sleep from which he did not awaken until there was a knock at his door.

Fredrik Ihlen stepped into Højbro's room.

"It is ten o'clock," he said. "But you do not have the day off from the bank today, do you?"

"Is it ten o'clock? No, I am not free."

Højbro jumped up.

"I have been dismissed from the *Gazette*. That is why I am at home."

"Yes, so I hear."

"Well, that's that. I suppose I should have taken your advice and left, but..."

"Oh, yes. But..."

"There is no longer any doubt about that."

Pause.

"You are already dressed. Were you up too early and decided to take a nap afterwards?" asked Ihlen.

"Yes, that's probably what happened."

"That has happened to me before, too. What I wanted to say is that you are in the *Gazette* again today."

"Oh yes."

And while Højbro was washing himself, Ihlen went in to fetch the paper. It was, in fact, merely the same article as last time, only more sharply worded. The charge of tainted business was more strongly emphasized. It had taken a definite form. There was no longer any question of any hearsay. God and everybody knew it. In his repetition, in his not letting a case go, but taking it up again day after day for more severe treatment, one could recognize the old Lynge again. Højbro read the notice with interest and did not say a word when he had finished.

"What do you say? What do you think?"

"It is said," Højbro replied, "about Actaeon, that once on a hunting expedition he surprised Artemis with her nymphs in the bath. As punishment for this involuntary offense, Artemis turned him into a deer, and her own hunting dogs tore him to pieces. So it is with me too. I have attacked Lynge in his element and written a pamphlet, and this pamphlet of mine now comes back to destroy me through Lynge. Ah well, what can one say?"

"No, what can one say?"

When Ihlen had gone, Højbro slapped his forehead several times as he paced to and fro in his room. Every time he came to the door he stopped for a second and listened for footsteps, but he heard none. Perhaps Charlotte was not up yet. Perhaps she had gone out already. He wrung his hands and begged in a whisper for her to come to him now. And the *Gazette*, it was after him again. It wrote brazenly about his reputation, as if it knew of a single blemish on it. There on the table was the money. It would take him but a few minutes to run down to the bank and pay his debt, and it would all be settled in half an hour, his honor saved, and the *Gazette*'s insinuations struck down forever.

What then? And Charlotte, the innocent, the lovely child! Suddenly he rushed to the table, seized the money, and quickly folded it up. Then he took out an envelope and put the notes in it. He stuck a card in after on which he had written a farewell, a thank you for everything, dear. Then he addressed the envelope to Charlotte and burned all his other letters. The table was cleared. Everything was in order. Charlotte's traveling money lay in the middle of the floor, on the dark carpet, so that it would be discovered immediately.

He rushed out of his room and reached the street without being seen. At the same moment, he cast his eyes up to the second floor and saw Charlotte's face. She backed away timidly. He took off his hat and saluted her, his dark face twitching, although he was smiling. She responded with a wave down to him, and when he continued to stand there looking up, she threw aside the curtain and stepped right up to the window. And he waved to her again.

Half an hour later Højbro handed himself over to the police.

XVIII

A couple of weeks later, the *Gazette*—the first with the news as always—announced in a warm, sympathetic notice that Fredrik Ihlen, the *Gazette*'s highly esteemed employee, had left for America. He had taken his sister with him, Miss Charlotte Ihlen, so well known in sporting circles. May it now go well for them in the new country! According to reports, Mr. Ihlen was in negotiations for a professorship at one of the American universities, and the *Gazette* wanted to congratulate America on its acquisition.

Thus Lynge showed his goodwill for Ihlen to the last. He himself smiled at this rumor about the professorship, which he had made up on his own, invented on the spot while writing the article. His playful nature was constantly at work in him, and shortened many a dull hour.

Lynge had, by the way, not shied away from serious issues either. The parliamentary elections were approaching, and Lynge had been campaigning in the field with election articles for several weeks. He had asserted the purest left-wing position with a bravery that set even the *Northman* completely back. Endre Bondesen had helped him. The young radical, who had actually made his debut as a verse writer, produced time after time very useful election articles, full of true feeling and power. Lynge was very grateful for this help, as he was no longer as quick with the pen as before and could certainly do with a helping hand. His old agility was gone, and his blows were becoming more and more like the *Northman*'s, blows from which no man would ever stagger. But did he rest? Not at all. On the contrary, Lynge toiled more fiercely than ever. In the midst of his declining journalistic abilities, he worked diligently as if nothing was more important in his life than that the Liberal Party would triumph in the upcoming election. No one could complain about his faith in the cause and his willingness to defend it this time. Every day the *Gazette* published an election editorial. Only Birkeland, the mill owner, was alone in his shadowy suspicion and said: "Even if Lynge writes pure Liberal Party politics for ten years in a row without wavering, I will still not be convinced that he does not have an ulterior motive."

But Birkeland, as many good qualities as that man had, was one of the stubbornest men in the country. So many times he had stared, open-mouthed, at Lynge when this brilliant editor danced easily through his difficulties. Birkeland could not understand how he did it, and he merely repeated his dubious phrase about the ten years and the ulterior motive, which he, unfortunately, got fewer and fewer people to agree with.

Lynge was able to convince the public that his past political meanderings were not that serious. He was as good as any Norwegian leftist when the going got tough. True, he had switched positions at times, but he himself had realized that he ought not to have done so, and many a time in private he sat down to bitterly regret these changes which had proved so unfortunate. Why, he could have been knocked off his perch! He had almost been left out of the whole game by a hair's breadth. And Lynge did not want to be left out. He still felt all the possibilities of the world within him, and could accomplish more than anyone realized.

Had not he just now celebrated a new triumph in the Højbro affair? Lynge had felt in his blood that Højbro was the kind of person in society who was ripe for exposure, and he had not needed to direct more than the occasional nasty jab at him before he surrendered.

At the same time, he was able to surprise the country with a complete list of the nominated jury officials several days before the appointments took place. This great coup caused a quite a bit of excitement, and people again said that Lynge could be blamed for one thing and another, but he had no equal. The coups had been a success, and Lynge rubbed his hands with satisfaction over these new victories. And would he be knocked off his perch? Never! Never!

A messenger arrived from the Left's headquarters with a letter, and a reply was requested.

Lynge ran through the letter and replied immediately. The Liberal Party Association wished to reprint some of his election articles in a special publication, and distribute tens of thousands of copies around the country. Of course, he gladly gave permission for this. The articles were at their full disposal, absolutely free of charge, for the sake of the Fatherland. He gave the messenger a crown. It was a young messenger, a boy with blue eyes who had probably never before seen Editor Lynge in his chair.

"Here you are! Buy yourself a picture book."

Touched by the boy's gratitude, Lynge jumped up and searched through his piles of paper for some illustrated magazines and periodicals, which he also handed to him. This letter from the Liberal Party Association had great significance for him at that moment and made him very happy. His tireless election work was recognized and appreciated, and the Association would not have wanted to reprint the *Gazette*'s articles unless they felt they were worth it. Now he wanted to write another article precisely for this special edition. He wanted to do it at once, and already had the subject in mind.

Then Leporello poked his head in the door.

It seemed that always when Lynge was busily occupied, Leporello came. Lynge no longer had much use for him. He did not need his help as often as before. Also, he secretly suspected Leporello of having gossiped, giving Højbro intimate information for his pamphlet. Lynge was upset at this thought. Had he deserved such faithlessness? He had observed an unknown woman in the street one day, and his first thought had been to set Leporello to work inquiring about her, but fortunately, he had thought better of it, and had only uttered a few vague words. He was not a young man anymore. His forty years were no age for joking. His fire was waning, and he needed his little remnant of passion for the newspaper. He had lately begun to spend more time at home in the evenings. He now read manuscripts thoroughly, provided them with headlines, and fiddled with scraps and notes as diligently as an ant. In the morning he could then look back on a job well done.

"The lady you were talking about the other day is called Madam Olsen," said Leporello.

Lynge looked up from his desk.

"Yes, let her be called Madam Olsen as much as she likes," he replied. "I'm not that curious anymore. It just occurred to me to ask you if you knew her." But Leporello, who also knew his editor and knew how to give him information in a roundabout way, answered quickly:

"Of course. But isn't it curious: her husband has a hawker's shop in the district. He deals with all the loose girls in the district, and do you know what they call him? These girls have given him the name of the Prince of Feathers. Hahaha."

Lynge smiled a little reluctantly. He would have preferred to be rid of Leporello today. But Leporello was, against his custom, very talkative, and asked:

"What new man have you got in the office?"

It was the new poet, the genius from Tordenskjoldsgade. Lynge had taken him in and helped him get started on the right footing. He was interested in developing this talent. "That is the new Norwegian poet. Take a look at him on your way out." And Lynge nodded his head in the direction of the door.

But Leporello ignored this hint and did not go. Out of habit, he began to tell Lynge what he had heard in the streets and cafés. The town was talking about the *Gazette* again. People found it better, the election articles, the articles about the Jæren Railway, the notices about the murder in Rakkestad, and the sinking at Tvedestrand. Everything was just fine. There was something for everyone. The *Gazette*'s warm-hearted proposal for women to be allowed to become state auditors had produced a veritable shout of jubilation in the progressive camp. Now, once and for all, it was finally the end of this talk that women could not be equal to men when such a powerful organ as the *Gazette* had made itself an advocate for women's election to public office.

It exhilarated Lynge to hear these statements. He was filled with satisfaction, with mild pleasure, and when he realized that Leporello would hardly leave before he had had a crown or two for dinner, he handed him a small banknote with a benevolent smile and nodded.

After Leporello had gone, Lynge remained sitting there leaning back in his chair, with his eyes fixed on his little shelf of encyclopedic works. The *Gazette* sailed up in the wind again, and the subscribers were coming back. And why not? Anyone who could read had to recognize that his was really the only paper in the country. It was no longer as white-hot as before, no, but it had one more advantage: it could be read in every home, by every young lady. Lynge had again spoken out for an improvement in the tone of the press, and he had done so in the name of good taste.

All spring he had been putting one excellent idea after another into his newspaper. No sooner had the snow disappeared than he again began his articles on sports. He even announced a year-round sports journal, to be published even in winter when skis and skates were in use. In all fields, he established his position, becoming the city's ultimate authority. The idea of women as state auditors had really been a happy whim of his, and more were still to follow. He would introduce a tax on walking sticks. Every man who was not compelled by bodily infirmity to use a walking stick should pay a certain annual sum to gain access to one. On every passenger ship on the coast and fjords, he wanted to have a tombola.* During the tourist season, it would be a welcome pastime for the many travelers to amuse themselves with this tombola, the proceeds of which would go to the Tourist Association, which in turn would use them for advertising. He also wanted to draw attention to the pictures on the Norwegian playing cards. Were they pictures worthy to be put on one's whist table? What if they simply printed cards with the country's most famous men and women on them, the greatest artists, politicians, and poets? In short, national playing cards with famous and important faces on them. The *Gazette* would gladly open a campaign in which the whole country could participate. Those who received the most votes would be designated kings, queens, and jacks respectively. A week later, Lynge thought of tightening the legislation regarding the protection of animals. In the summer, when the villagers traveled to the country, they left their cats in town, chased them out into the street, shut the doors on them, and let them starve. Shouldn't there be a stop to this?

There really wasn't a hole too narrow for Lynge to drill into and come back with an interesting idea. When you added to this all the artists and witty minds who wrote informative and humorous pieces for the *Gazette*, it was not the least bit surprising that the paper was read with eagerness everywhere.

Endre Bondesen stopped in, delivered a manuscript, and at the same time wanted to draw the editor's attention to a mistake. It was not Charlotte Ihlen who had accompanied her brother to America. It was Sofie, her sister.

"Are you sure about that?" Lynge asked.

"Absolutely certain. I have seen Charlotte today in the street. I

---

*Translator's note: A game of chance in which a numbered ticket is pulled from a spinning container and a small prize is won when the number matches that of the player's ticket.

have also heard that it was originally Charlotte who was to have traveled with him, but for certain reasons she stayed back."

"For what reasons?"

"I don't really know. although I've heard it had something to do with Højbro, Leo Højbro. I don't really know."

Lynge considered the matter. He did not like to make corrections. He corrected as little as possible. That was his principle. What had been published in the *Gazette* had been published, and that was that. But when Bondesen had gone, Lynge saved himself with a very simple addition, a new note: Miss Charlotte Ihlen, who had accompanied her brother and sister some distance on the road, as announced, had returned.

And again he was interrupted as he was about to begin his latest election article. Kongsvold, the Ministry man, poked his thin, worn-out face in the door.

Lynge looked at him a little puzzled. Kongsvold greeted him. He had always before been reserved, almost a little self-conscious. Now he smiled even more humbly, offered his hand to Lynge, and in general behaved like a man who wanted sympathy. The poor devil had nothing else on his mind than that the head of the Ministry had gotten wind of his connection with the publication of the famous jury nominations and had now as good as given him a hint to seek his way out of the Ministry.

Lynge listened to this very confidential affair with patience.

"How the hell could anyone suspect that it was you who was my source?" he asked. "It did not come from us."

"No, I don't understand it," replied Kongsvold.

And he humbly and sadly tilted his head and repeated once more that he did not understand it.

"You have obviously been careless in one way or another. Such things take their revenge."

Careless? No, no, he had not been careless. But there was the fact that he and he alone had the nominations in his hands to dispatch them.

Well, it was a sorry story.

Yes, it was.

But it wasn't really that serious, was it?

Kongsvold was certain of his situation. He had been given a clear hint to start looking for another profession.

Lynge turned back to his desk. He certainly had no advice for him, regrettably.

"It is very unfortunate," Lynge said.

Pause.

"Yes, I don't know what to do," said Kongsvold, quietly and cautiously.

Lynge did not reply to this.

"I don't know at all. I thought I'd ask you."

"What about?"

"Well, what I should do, what I should come up with."

"No, of course, you must decide for yourself what to do in this matter. It would not be good for me to tell you what to do or not to do."

These words made Kongsvold's head sink still deeper, and he stared forlornly at the floor.

"If I looked for another position now, I don't think I'd be able to get one," he said. "I'm unlikely to get a recommendation from the State Council."

"No, it may not be so easy for you to find something else."

"Yes, you would help me in that case, wouldn't you?"

"Of course, what little I can, but you know yourself that in the administration we have now, they don't even read my paper, so my help wouldn't bear much fruit."

"Well, at least do what you can."

"No, to put it bluntly, I think you would be poorly served by that," replied Lynge. "It would be even more obvious to everyone that we had worked together if I gave my support to you now. Don't you realize that?"

And at once Kongsvold realized this too. He had to agree with Lynge. He sat there for several minutes without saying anything. But suddenly a bright spark shot down into his soul. He would go to his boss and tell him everything. He would ask for mercy this time and promise to never again abuse his position. Who knows? The boss might listen to him!

He got up quietly and said goodbye.

"Farewell!" replied Lynge. And he turned again to his desk and began to write his election article. It was important to complete this special edition, this excellent series of articles which was to bring the Liberal Party victory among Norway's voters. One did one's duty and fought for one's cause, and Birkeland could speculate as much as he liked about the ten years and the ulterior motive.

Acknowledgments

Thanks to Brian Skillin for lending his proofreading expertise to this project. And thanks to the following for their generous financial support which helped to defray some of this publication's production costs:

Thomas Young Barmore Jr, Nick Barry, Melissa Beck, ARNELA BEKTAS, Joseph Benincase, Cameron Bennett, Sam Bertram, Matthew Boe, Brian R. Boisvert, Tom Bowden, Michael Chen, Scott Chiddister, Adam Cipriani, Alex Cobb, Seth Coblentz, Eric L. Collette, Joshua Lee Cooper, S COSTA, Tim Crain, Parker & Malcolm Curtis, R Eggleton, Isaac Ehrlich, John Feins, Thomas Gagnon, Justin Gallant, garyrasp@att.net, Finn Gaustad, GMarkC, R. V. Goodson, Damian Gordon, B. F. Gordon, Jr., David Greenberg, Geoffrey Greene, Tim H, Everett Haagsma, Elizabeth O. Hackler, Aric Herzog, David Holets, J. Holmes, Conor Hultman, Neil Glenn Jacobson, Fred W Johnson, Jacob H Joseph, Alex Juarez, Anthony Kozak, Mark Lamb, Scott J Lawrie, Jim McElroy, Donald McGowan, BT McMenomy, Alan James mc Quillan, Jack Mearns, William Messing, Jason H Miller, Jody Mock, Gregory Moses, Scott Murphy, Michael O'Shaughnessy, Dian Parker, Andrew Pearson, Julie Phillips, Pedro Ponce, Judith Redding in memory of Jean Pearson, Mahesh Reddy, Ryan C. Reeves, Terry E Roberts, K. Seifried, Bill Shute, Mindie and Drew Simmons, Robert E. Slaven, K.L. Stokes, Aurora Sun, Stephen Tabler, S. Taushanoff, Edmund Vosik,

Eris Wadham, William Walsh, Rachel Wells, Isaiah Whisner, Charles Wilkins, Brad Wojak, T.R. Wolfe, Beth Worley, Kale Worsham, The Zemenides Family, and Anonymous